MOMENT OF REUNION, MOMENT OF TRUTH

Kyodai Ken stepped in with a python's speed. He grabbed Bruce Wayne and hurled him through the air. Bruce smacked into a pile of woven baskets, sending them scattering with the impact as he thrashed on the floor. The Ninja sneered at his struggling foe, hands on hips. "You have lost all your skill, Wayne!" he crowed. "Even a white belt could have avoided that throw."

Summer Gleeson shook her head as Bruce climbed slowly to his feet. "Stop it! Can't you see he's no match for you?"

"But that's the joke, woman." The Ninja advanced in a slow, creeping fashion, his legs splayed. "He never was!"

BATMAN™

The Animated Series

THE DRAGON AND THE BAT

A Novelization by
GEARY GRAVEL

BANTAM BOOKS

NEW YORK   TORONTO   LONDON

SYDNEY   AUCKLAND

THE DRAGON AND THE BAT

A Bantam Spectra Book / June 1994

Produced by RHK Creative Services

Based on the scripts Night of the Ninja *by Steve Perry and* Day of the Samurai *by Steve Perry.*

SPECTRA *and the portrayal of a boxed "s" are trademarks
of Bantam Books,
a division of Bantam Doubleday Dell Publishing Group, Inc.*

BATMAN *and all related characters, slogans, and indicia are
trademarks of DC Comics.*

Batman created by Bob Kane.

ISBN 0-553-56608-3

Published simultaneously in the United States and Canada
*This book is intended for sale only in the United States of America,
its territories and dependencies, the Republic of the Philippines, and
Canada*

Bantam Books are published by Bantam Books, a division of Bantam
Doubleday Dell Publishing Group, Inc. Its trademark, consisting of the
words "Bantam Books" and the portrayal of a rooster, is Registered in
U.S. Patent and Trademark Office and in other countries. Marca
Registrada. Bantam Books, 1540 Broadway, New York, New York
10036.

PRINTED IN THE UNITED STATES OF AMERICA

OPM   0 9 8 7 6 5 4 3 2 1

For
Tom Kidd
Nick Jainschigg
Dave Deitrick
Paul Chadwick
Rick Berry

uncompromising artists,
good friends,
and sterling fellows

THE DRAGON AND THE BAT

1

Night lay like a sweltering blanket over Gotham City.

Darkness had done nothing to dispel the heat of the day, and the heavy humidity lent a slightly blurred, unreal appearance to ordinary things that had people blinking and looking again. Certain Gotham sights, however, inspired a second look under the best of conditions.

The rooftop of the tall building located at the corner of Cugel Street and Vance Avenue had been constructed to resemble a huge, stylized makeup case. At one end, a colossal red lipstick rotated slowly up and down in a golden tube the size of a missile silo. Next to it, a fifteen-foot compact opened like a giant clam shell to reveal a Mylar-coated mirror and a powder puff that could have doubled as a queen-sized bed. A water tower disguised as a perfume atomizer sprayed clouds of unnecessary mist into the damp night air of an early summer heat wave.

At the base of the display a rectangular black sign bore the words "Wayne Cosmetics" in angular, yard-high gilt letters. "A Subsidiary of Wayne Enterprises" appeared below in smaller script.

It was nearly midnight. Several yards below the mammoth lipstick, a single office window still gleamed with fluorescent light. Inside, the heavy-set night manager sat hunched forward at his desk, his eyes squinting at the rows of glowing letters appearing on the monitor of his computer. His fingers raced across the keyboard as he completed the memo. He stopped typing and leaned back, scanning the monitor critically. Then he made one or two minor changes to the text, gave a small nod of satisfaction, and punched the key that would activate the printer.

The night manager raised his head with a frown in the seconds before the noisy clacking began in the corner of the room. He had heard something that sounded like a faint hiss coming from the direction of the hall doorway. He swiveled in his seat and stared uncomprehending at the cloud of purple gas billowing in under the closed door.

"What the—?"

He pushed to his feet, then clutched at his throat, coughing. The chair springs squeaked loudly above the printer noise as he slumped back, unconscious.

Precisely twenty-five seconds later, the door to the hallway eased open, purple gas swirling in its wake. The printer finished chattering to itself on the other side of the room and fell silent.

The man who stepped lightly into the room was clad in form-fitting black from the top of his head to the soles of his feet. An angled cutout exposed his eyes. He wore a red sash around his waist, and the hilt of a slender sword protruded from an ornate sheath at his side.

Glancing briefly at the unconscious night manager, the intruder stepped across the room to a large wall safe. He pulled a small mechanism from inside his suit and attached it to the front of the safe.

A tiny red light winked on as the device hummed to life. The man in black set his gloved hand carefully on the safe's dial. He spun the knob slowly back and forth, watching intently as the red light on the side of the little box was replaced several times by a green one. Finally the device made a cheeping noise and the intruder tugged at the dial. He made a small sound of satisfaction as the safe door opened smoothly outward.

Inside were stacks of cash and negotiable bonds. He removed them from the safe and stuffed them into a small brown sack, then tucked the end of the sack under his scarlet sash.

The man in black moved to the night manager's desk. Shoving the chair and its occupant to one side, he leaned forward to study the computer. He produced a small disk from inside his suit, inserted it into the hard drive, and typed a quick command on the keyboard.

He held his breath.

The monitor went blank for a few seconds. Then it flashed to life, the screen filling with columns of numbers that scrolled endlessly upward.

Thirty seconds later, the computer made a beeping noise. The parade of numerals halted, several lines now glowing brighter than the rest.

The man in black smiled. *"Yoku dekimashita,"* he murmured. "Well done." His black-gloved fingers stroked the keyboard.

The screen began to flash: WARNING! WARNING! THIS COMMAND WILL DAMAGE THE SYSTEM!

The intruder tapped out a final confirmation of his order. The screen flashed persistently for another twenty seconds, then the words SYSTEMS FAILURE appeared, and the monitor went dark.

The black-clad man paused to pull a small air filter from beneath his mask and stow it inside his suit. Then he rolled the unconscious night manager back up to his desk and bowed ironically at the slack-jawed figure. *"Domo arigato,"* he said softly.

He was padding silently toward the half-open door when he heard a noise in the corridor. He extinguished the lights in the office and flattened against the wall. Moments later a yellow oval of light shone into the office. The intruder drew his sword from its sheath and raised it above his head in both hands.

A hand holding a flashlight appeared in the darkened doorway. The sword flashed down.

There was a cry of surprise as the blade sliced cleanly through the barrel of the flashlight and the room was plunged into darkness again. The man in black darted out the door past the astonished guard and raced down the long corridor.

The metal ladder was where his research had told him it would be.

Moments later, he emerged through a narrow hatchway onto the surface of the roof. The giant cosmetics case loomed in dark silhouette above him. A rope hung down into the darkness over the edge of the roof, its end fixed to a stanchion at the bottom of the perfume tower. The intruder slipped wraithlike to the top of the rope, securing the sack at his waist as he prepared to climb down. He lifted his head at a crunch of gravel.

"Hey—you!" A second guard peered across the rooftop from the base of the lipstick's golden silo. The guard fumbled with something in her hand and a wide beam of yellow light swept across the roof. "Who's there?"

The rooftop was silent. The guard squinted at the complicated shadows cast by the movement of the massive makeup implements. She shone her flashlight beam into the slowly opening compact. Had she really seen someone or—

Something small and shiny came whirring toward her through the air. The sound seemed to come from several directions at once. The guard spun around in surprise when the first of the throwing stars pinned her jacket at the shoulder to the heavy canvas of the simulated powder puff. "What on—"

Chok-chok-chok. Three more of the razor-sharp weapons followed, fastening her securely at shoulders and waist. She struggled vainly, the flashlight dropping from her hand. The sharp metal teeth had bit deep into the wooden frame of the giant mock-up. As the guard looked wildly around the rooftop, a small sound drew her gaze to the perfume atomizer.

A black silhouette stood just behind the cloud of cloying vapor. She blinked. When the mist dissipated, the edge of the roof was empty.

2

The gymnasium was large, well lit, and stocked with state-of-the-art equipment. Rows of gleaming machines alternated with racks of carefully arranged free weights along the mirrored walls. Thick workout mats covered a portion of the floor. At the center of one of the mats, two men prepared to face each other in battle.

Both combatants wore the loose white pants and the white jacket known as a *gi* commonly employed in karate. The older man had dark hair and an expression of calm concentration on his ruggedly handsome face. His *gi* was clasped by a black belt. The gym, the palatial manor in which it sat, and the exquisitely landscaped estate that surrounded the mansion, belonged to him. The man's name was Bruce Wayne, and in addition to being a billionaire and the head of a powerful corporate conglomerate, he was also a martial arts expert.

"When you're ready." Bruce exchanged a bow with the other man as the two assumed their sparring stances.

Bruce's opponent wore a brown belt over his *gi*. His youthful face shone with anticipation under its tousle of dark hair. The younger man's name was Dick Grayson. He had been Bruce's ward since the age of nine, when his parents had fallen to their deaths from the high wire at the circus where they were employed as aerialists. Dick grinned at the older man, measuring him with his eyes for a long moment. Then, without warning, he leaped at Bruce, his hands extended with palms rigid. *"Hai!"*

Bruce's expression remained calm. He stood as if rooted to the mat. At the last moment, his arms came up. He whirled in a split-second aikido-type turn and threw the younger man smoothly into the air.

"Oof!" Dick tucked his head to hit the mat in a headfirst dive, managed an awkward shoulder roll, and came up into a sitting position.

Bruce stood looking down at him, arms folded on his chest. "Did you get it?"

Dick combed his fingers back through his dark hair. He gave a shaky nod. "I think so."

"Show me."

The young man rose fluidly to his feet and assumed the fighting stance. "My pleasure," he said with a smile. "When *you're* ready."

Bruce seemed to relax, his eyelids drooping slightly. Then suddenly he was in motion, a black-and-white blur in the air as he leaped toward Dick. The younger man whirled around, arms moving rapidly as he attempted to duplicate the defensive move Bruce had used on him.

He almost pulled it off.

This time Dick Grayson landed on his back, slapping the mat with the flat of his palms to absorb the force of the fall.

Bruce stood above him again, his breathing even. "Not quite," he said.

"Sorry." Dick got to his feet more slowly this time, the eager grin replaced by a rueful half smile. "Some of us aren't perfect, I guess," he said with a slight edge to his voice.

"Master Bruce?" The elderly man who stood in the doorway of the gym was prim and poised, the epitome of British butlership in his black tails and bow tie. "Sorry to interrupt," Alfred Pennyworth said to his employer, "but Lucius Fox just telephoned from the main office. I'm afraid there has been another robbery at a Wayne Enterprises company."

"Whoa!" Dick wiped the back of his sleeve across his sweaty brow. "That's the sixth one in less than two weeks!"

Bruce gave his head a small shake. "Seventh," he said grimly. He raised his brows to the butler. "Where did they hit this time, Alfred?"

3

The giant makeup kit that topped the roof of
Wayne Cosmetics had been strung with yellow police tape, giving it an almost festive
look.

Commissioner James Gordon of the
Gotham City Police had the feeling he was in
the middle of a bizarre theme park as he eyed the
outsize props. He was standing next to the giant
compact, whose opening and closing mechanism
had been temporarily shut off. The night guard's
brown jacket still hung from the simulated powder puff, pinned to the wood by four star-shaped
metal objects. Next to the commissioner stood
Henry Texiera, night manager of Wayne Cosmetics.

"Unfortunately, I didn't see anything at all,"
Texiera said as Gordon examined the scene. "I
was down in my office writing up the closing report on the computer. Next thing I know, I'm
waking up in the hospital with a headache." He
patted his cap of close-cropped black hair gingerly. "Still throbs a bit."

"The first guard didn't get a look at him either. The second one told us it was a big man dressed in black." Gordon leaned down to inspect one of the throwing stars. "It's the same guy, all right. It's got to be." He looked up as Bruce Wayne crossed the roof to join them.

"Henry." Bruce nodded to the night manager. "I want you to take the rest of the day off, as soon as they're finished with you." He turned to Gordon. "Good morning, Commissioner."

"I wish," Gordon muttered. He stepped to one side so that Bruce could see the jacket. "At least something more than unconscious Wayne employees was left behind this time." He pointed a blunt fingertip at the quartet of metal objects. A small, intricate design had been etched into the surface of each of them. "Mean anything to you?"

Bruce leaned in and inspected the nearest object. He recognized it instantly as a *shuriken*, the throwing star employed by Japanese martial artists. Then he looked more closely at the etched lines. The design was a stylized dragon, coiling menacingly around the central opening in the star. Bruce's eyes narrowed, his mind racing backward through the years. . . .

4

A rack of gleaming *shuriken* had dominated one wall of the main dojo in the spare and traditional martial arts school presided over by Master Yoru. A sheathed longsword known as a *daito* rested on an elaborately carved wooden stand in front of the throwing stars. An elderly Japanese man sat with half a dozen students on *tatami* mats, their attention glued to the match that was taking place in the center of the dojo.

Clad in white *gi* and trousers, the young Bruce Wayne was sparring with a Japanese man of similar size and build. As Bruce flung himself forward in a spirited attack, the other man whirled into an aikido-like turn. His hands seemed to come from nowhere as he tossed Bruce easily through the air. The young American landed on the padded floor and rolled to a sitting position, his face burning.

The Japanese man strode to Bruce's side and extended his hand to help his fallen opponent, a look of exaggerated sympathy on his handsome features. Bruce ignored the gesture, hopping to his feet and brushing off his *gi* with angry sweeps of his hands.

The elderly instructor uncrossed his legs and rose from the mat.

"The match is over," Master Yoru said quietly. "Kyodai Ken is the victor."

Kyodai clucked his tongue. "Don't be depressed, Wayne-*san*," he said. "You are not a bad fighter for a pampered rich man's son." He flashed an arrogant smile. "I, however, am better."

The old man flowed onto the sparring mat like quicksilver. A moment later, Kyodai Ken was lying on his back on the mat, the elderly master standing over him with his hands on his hips.

"There is *always* someone better, Kyodai Ken," Master Yoru said sternly. "Now apologize to your classmate for your insulting remark."

Kyodai ran a palm over his shaven skull and sat up, glaring at Bruce. "My apologies," he said stiffly.

"Besting another is easy," Yoru commented as his pupil climbed sullenly to his feet. "Besting yourself is much harder."

Kyodai bowed and turned away, his face still flushed from the rebuke. He pulled off his *gi* and wiped his face with it. Bruce's gaze was drawn to his classmate's back, and to the intricately rendered tattoo of a coiled dragon that stretched from his waist to his neck. . . .

"Mr. Wayne?"

The sun had almost reached its zenith. The temperature on the rooftop was rising steadily.

Bruce raised his hand unconsciously and wiped at his brow, the image of the dragon still burning behind his eyes.

"Mr. Wayne? Hello?"

Bruce shook his head and looked up to see newswoman Summer Gleeson standing directly in front of him, a look of impatience on her attractive features. Behind her, a young man with a red baseball cap and a blond ponytail balanced an expensive-looking minicam on his shoulder. "Okay, Joe, I think we've got his attention now." Summer signaled the cameraman to follow as she stepped forward, a tiny microphone extended in the direction of Bruce's chin.

"Do you have any idea why someone has been systematically burglarizing and sabotaging businesses belonging to you?" Summer paused while Joe swung his camera around to take in her earnest expression. "Two buildings burned to the ground, another partially blown up—and the computer system in this one rendered useless—"

"Excuse me." Commissioner Gordon elbowed his way past the cameraman. He turned to glare at the auburn-haired newswoman. "Ms. Gleeson, would you mind telling me how you came into possession of that last piece of information?"

"Oh, a good reporter has her sources, Commissioner." She dismissed him with a charming smile and turned back to Bruce. "Any thoughts, Mr. Wayne? Any comment on what's behind this apparent vendetta against you and Wayne Enterprises?" She beckoned the blond cameraman, who squeezed past Gordon with an apologetic expression till the lens of his minicam hovered six inches from Bruce's profile.

Bruce shied away from the camera as if it could sting him. "If you'll excuse me . . ." He turned on his heel and strode off across the roof.

Summer Gleeson let the microphone droop in her hand. "You can't ignore the press forever, Mr. Wayne," she called after him. She put her hand on the cameraman's elbow and guided him off in the opposite direction. "C'mon, Joe. I'd say it's time to come down off the roof and do a little digging. . . ."

5

The cavern was vast. Large portions of it remained in undisturbed darkness, while isolated areas glowed under cones of white light from the high-powered lamps located strategically among the forest of stalactites. The near-silent hum of expensive instruments blended with the muted sibilance of leathery wings, as the majority of the cave's denizens dozed peacefully beneath its vaulted ceiling.

The cavern's two human inhabitants stood on a plateau of natural rock that had been fitted with a twenty-foot turntable. A vehicle sat on the turntable like a model in a futuristic display, its sleek black curves glinting with reflected light.

"Will there be anything else, Master Bruce?" Alfred Pennyworth passed a supple band of gleaming gold to the man who stood next to the vehicle, then watched as the other man clasped it around his waist.

"No, thank you, Alfred." The buckling mechanism came together with a sharp click. Beneath the gold belt, the man wore a form-fitting costume of gray and blue-black, with a long, scalloped black cape that stirred like a restless wing in the breeze from the ventilators. A black cowl crowned his head with two jutting points, and a black mask concealed the upper half of his face. The gold emblem on his broad chest bore the stylized image of a bat suspended in flight.

"I may be home quite late," the man in the costume added. He turned to the waiting vehicle.

"Very good, sir." As Alfred began to back away from the circular platform, a pulse of light in the tall, cylindrical structure that clung to the cavern's wall caught his eye. He cleared his throat as the costumed man began to climb into the fantastic car. "Is there any message you would like me to give Master Dick?"

Batman frowned over his shoulder as the pulse of light reached ground level and a curving door slid open.

"Hey!" Dick Grayson emerged from the tubular elevator. He covered the distance to the Batmobile at a brisk trot. "Wait up. I was gonna join you tonight, remember? This might be my last chance for a couple of months. You know I'm due to start my summer gig at Haly's Circus day after tomorrow."

The man in the black mask settled into the driver's seat with a shake of his head. "Sorry."

Dick looked dismayed. "Listen, I know I should've been down here sooner, but my old roomie Brian called. He's doing a football clinic for inner city kids up at State and wants to hitch a ride when I head out for Haly's." He half turned back toward the main plateau. "It'll take me two minutes to get into my costume—"

"Not this time, Dick."

"But—"

Batman depressed a switch and the transparent canopy slid into place above his head. The engine roared to life, and the Batmobile zoomed up the ramp on a tail of fire.

"What's with him this time, Alfred?" The young man turned to the butler with a scowl of frustration. "Did he wake up on the wrong side of the belfry?"

Alfred gave a noncommittal shrug. "You know Master Bruce. He's not one to discuss his feelings."

"Ain't that the truth." Dick stared after the departed vehicle in dissatisfaction. "He must be going to investigate those attacks on Wayne Enterprises. Something's eating him big time about this case, Alfred. I don't know what it is—and since he won't tell me . . ." His words trailed off, a look of calculation replacing the frown.

Alfred clucked his tongue. "Master Dick, wouldn't it be more advisable to respect his wishes in this matter and remain at home? You know, I've a rather interesting game of strategy I've been wanting to show you. It was developed by the Japanese, and utilizes a number of black and white pebbles to represent the capture and loss of territory." The butler raised his brows hopefully at the young man. "I could prepare us some fresh orangeade. . . ."

"Pebbles?" Dick looked skeptical. "Alfred, you know as well as he does that *this* is the only game that's gonna hold my attention—at least until I've figured out what's going on." Leaving the empty platform, he mounted a series of shallow steps toward another, smaller turntable. He lifted a black helmet from the back of the streamlined black motorcycle that occupied the platform and tossed it lightly to the butler. "Keep an eye on this for me till I get into my work clothes, will you? Oh, and orangeade sounds great for later—just don't start squeezing till you see the whites of our eyes!"

Alfred cradled the shiny helmet in his arms with a sigh.

6

The Batmobile hurtled like a black comet down the back roads toward Gotham City. The Dark Knight eased up on the accelerator when he entered the sweltering city. Well-trained muscles and reflexes allowed him to operate the futuristic vehicle with mechanical perfection as he cruised the night streets. His thoughts once more drifted back through time . . .

Bruce had been alone in Master Yoru's dojo that night, practicing the stylized martial arts poses known as katas with a grim intensity. Perspiration shone on his face as he shifted fluidly from one stance to another. After a while he turned his attention to the *makawara* dummy suspended from the ceiling and began to savage it with kicks and punches, each one wringing a grunt of exertion from his lips.

"You practice as if driven by demons."

Master Yoru had entered silently. He stood in the doorway, stroking the white wisps of his beard as he observed his pupil. Bruce stepped away from the dummy and bowed to the master, his brow beaded with sweat.

"I am not good enough, Yoru *Sensei,*" he said, panting slightly. His lips compressed to a hard, straight line. "I *lost* today."

Yoru approached him. "Everyone loses now and again, Bruce-*san*. Everyone. To be a true warrior, one must learn to accept defeat as well as victory."

Bruce shook his head. "I *have* to be the best there is," he said simply. "No matter what it takes. Defeat is unacceptable."

"Yet defeat can sometimes be more instructive than victory," Yoru replied, quietly adamant. "And learning is always acceptable."

Batman gave the wheel a sharp turn to the left, frowning at the memory. He headed down a shadowy alleyway several blocks from the imposing skyscraper that served as the international headquarters for Wayne Enterprises. He exited the Batmobile, then turned and aimed a small remote control device at its gleaming cockpit. Instantly metal plates slid forth from concealed housings to cover the Batmobile in a sheath of impregnable black armor.

The Dark Knight fired his grappling gun at the nearest rooftop. The three-pronged hook fastened itself to the edge of the roof, its slender line growing taut. He pressed a stud on the side of the gun and was reeled silently into the air.

Batman covered the rest of the distance to Wayne Enterprises in his own unique fashion, slipping over rooftops and swooping like a silent raptor above the dark spaces between the buildings.

Finally he reached his destination, high above the city. The rooftop of the towering building appeared empty. The Dark Knight stood in the midst of an eerie, uninhabited landscape of ventilator ducts, massive air-conditioning units, and microwave relays. Nothing moved. There was no sound other than the purring thrum of the air conditioners.

"You might as well show yourself," Batman said. "I know you're here. It's only logical that Wayne's corporate headquarters would be your next target."

Nothing happened for the space of a heartbeat. Two. Three. Could he have been wrong?

Then a figure clad in black emerged like a wraith from the darkness behind the largest air-conditioning unit.

"So." The intruder gave a small bow, his eyes studying the Dark Knight. "The famous Batman. I am honored." His voice was deep, and his English was pronounced with a noticeable accent. "My business is not with you, however. Therefore I present you with two choices." Muscles contracted beneath the form-fitting black uniform as the relaxed posture shifted smoothly into an alert battle stance. "Walk away and live—or stay and be destroyed. It is all one to me."

Six feet away on the gravel-surfaced roof, the Dark Knight assumed a fighting stance that mirrored that of the intruder. As if responding to an unheard signal, the two men began to circle the invisible midpoint between them, shifting easily through a succession of offensive and defensive poses as each took the measure of the other.

"Hai!"

The intruder made the first move, leaping like a black panther across the rooftop. Batman's gray-clad figure seemed to waver like smoke as he feinted back, then stepped forward, tripping his attacker with a small motion of his leg.

The man in black turned his fall into a gymnast's tumble. He rolled swiftly to a standing position, twisting to face his foe just in time to counter the Dark Knight's first offensive. The foreign warrior's arms moved in a blur through the hazy summer air, and Batman reeled backward. Caught off balance, the Dark Knight contracted his body into a tucked front flip, landed with a crunch of boots on the gravel, and spun around.

The two men faced off once more, still as statues, as they evaluated each other through narrowed eyes.

Then the duel began again, lightning fast, an intricate martial dance whose individual encounters lasted no more than a fraction of a second. Slowly, relentlessly, Batman drove the other man back across the rooftop. As the masked intruder retreated under the Dark Knight's offensive, he reached inside his black garment and pulled forth a slim tube of bamboo. Raising it to his lips, he pointed it toward Batman and puffed out his cheeks. A blinding cloud of purple vapor sprayed outward from the end of the tube.

Batman swirled his cape in front of his face to divert the gas. The action came an instant too late. He coughed, staggered, and dropped heavily to one knee, shaking his head violently in an effort to remain conscious.

Beneath the black mask, the intruder's lips drew back in a humorless smile. He pulled a short, straight sword from the sheath at his side and slowly advanced on his helpless opponent. Moonlight glinted off the bright steel as he raised the blade above Batman's bowed shoulders.

The Dark Knight struggled to lift his head. Through eyes blurred by moisture and swirls of purple gas, he saw the distorted reflection of his own face staring down at him from the poised sword. The twisted face rushed toward him.

A sound like a pulsating whistle broke the silence, as something dark whirred across the rooftop, striking the sword hard and knocking it from the grip of the startled intruder. The blade drove into the yielding material of the rooftop and stuck there, vibrating.

The Japanese warrior gave a cry of rage and spun around. A young man dressed in a dramatic costume of dark red and green stood at the edge of the roof.

"Listen, Captain Ginsu, the guy in the pointy mask is my buddy—and we don't skewer my buddies." Robin moved forward as the Dark Knight got groggily to his feet. "True, he doesn't always know how to treat his friends—but, hey, he dresses like a giant bat—y'gotta love 'im." The young man stood at his partner's side, facing the intruder with hands on hips. "So, shall we recap? *Nobody* gets to slice 'n' dice the big guy while I'm around—got it?"

The black-garbed warrior studied the two who faced him and came to a decision with a sharp nod of his head. "Another time, then." He gave a polite bow, then snatched his sword from the rooftop and sprang toward the edge of the building.

"Hey!" Robin raced after him. "I think a formal introduction's in order, don't you?" The intruder moved in a series of high hops that had the young crime fighter dodging back and forth to keep up. Behind him, Batman leaned against a spidery microwave unit, breathing in deep gasps as he watched the frantic pursuit.

The masked warrior reached the edge of the rooftop and stood poised for a moment, gazing downward. Robin lunged forward, his gloved hand closing on the back of the black suit. The intruder danced to one side along the roof edge, a portion of his shirt tearing away in Robin's hand to reveal an intricate dragon tattoo that stretched its coils the length of the warrior's back.

Batman's eyes widened. "Robin! Stop!"

The young man halted obediently as the intruder flipped over the edge of the roof. Peering down, he watched the black-garbed man climb headfirst down the building like a giant spider.

"Sheesh." Robin shook his head in disbelief. "How does he *do* that?"

He turned back from the edge and crossed the roof to Batman, offering the older man his arm for support. The Dark Knight was rubbing his eyes with one hand. He waved Robin off with the other and stepped away from the microwave unit. His movements were shaky.

"You okay?" Robin watched him with concern.

"I'm fine." Batman straightened, seeming to overcome the lingering effects of the gas by sheer willpower. "What are you doing here?"

Robin's mouth twisted in a wry grin. "You're welcome, partner," he said with mock sincerity. "Anytime."

Batman seemed about to speak. Then he turned away. "Come on," he said over his shoulder. "There's nothing more to do here."

Robin's expression was puzzled in the flash of passing lights as the Batmobile barreled toward the outskirts of Gotham City. "I'm not exactly up on my Japanese history, but I thought samurai lived by some sort of code of honor. That gas gun wasn't exactly according to Hoyle, was it?"

"He wasn't a samurai." Batman kept his eyes on the road. "He was a ninja. Samurai are warriors. Ninja are spies and assassins. Their only code is to get the job done." He swung the sleek vehicle onto a side road that led out into the countryside. "I know this ninja."

"Say what?" Robin blinked in surprise, turning to stare at the man behind the wheel. "From where?"

"He and Bruce Wayne were students of the same master, years ago in Japan. His name is Kyodai Ken." The face below the mask was grim. "He was a good student."

"Yeah?" Robin detected something unexpected in the Dark Knight's tone. "How good was he?"

"Good," Batman said tersely.

"I see. . . ." Robin nodded, hearing the unspoken concern in the simple word. He turned to watch the rushing shapes of trees through the glass canopy.

7

Summer Gleeson perched on the edge of the television news editor's desk, surrounded by a jumble of TV monitors and computers. She was sipping a mug of muddy coffee and scanning a hard-copy printout of a crime sheet bulletin.

"I'm sure there's more to these crimes against Wayne Enterprises than meets the eye," the newswoman mused. She pursed her lips and pushed a strand of auburn hair back from her cheek with the hand that held the mug. "What do we really know about Billionaire Bruce, after all? I've been trying to come up with something interesting on him all day. You know what I've found?" She tossed the crime sheet onto the blotter and picked up a handwritten list. "Support for inner city health clinics. Funding to erect homeless shelters and initiate vocational training for the unemployed. Grants to help preserve examples of 'endangered American cultural treasures'—in other words, some ramshackle circus that was about to go under." She dropped the list onto the crime sheet with a look of disgust. "It goes on and on.

One of the richest men on the planet, but he comes off like the ultimate Boy Scout. He's got to be hiding something." Summer eased out of the thicket of instrumentation and stood in front of the crowded desk. "I have a notion to pop over to the Wayne Charities reception tonight and see if I can't find a few answers there."

Paul Woodley ran a hand through his thinning hair. "You be careful, kid. Wayne's got mondo clout in Gotham City."

"Woodley, Woodley." Summer favored him with the indulgent smile teenagers reserve for an overprotective parent. "I'm a big girl, now—remember?"

"Go is a fascinating game, Master Dick—not only is it the oldest game in the world still enjoyed in its original form, it's actually become a way of life for literally thousands of people in the Far East and elsewhere. Its moves are subtle and beautiful in execution—yet I've heard its intricate strategies compared with the tactics employed during guerrilla warfare." Alfred Pennyworth was industriously polishing a collection of heirloom silver while he held forth, his keen eyes alert for the slightest hint of tarnish. He wore a dark blue apron over his impeccable butler's uniform. Dick Grayson lounged in the nearby doorway, an expression of brooding distraction replacing his usual good cheer.

"Alfred," the young man said abruptly, "do you know anything about the training Bruce went through in Japan?"

The butler glanced up from a gleaming butter

knife with a look of mild surprise. "Why, of course," he replied. "I was there the whole time. Lovely country." He set down the knife and reached for a sardine fork. "I especially liked the tea. And, as you know, the fascinating game which I was just describing actually originated in—"

"You ever hear of this martial arts classmate of Bruce's?" Dick picked up a cake server and twisted it idly, watching his face wink in and out of view. "Guy named Kyodai Kent?"

"Ken," Alfred corrected. "Oh, indeed." He added the little fork to the cleaned silverware on the table and took the server from Dick's hand. "He was the only student at Yoru *Sensei*'s dojo who was consistently able to defeat Master Bruce. Unfortunately, he had a rather . . . flexible code of honor." The butler's prim features tightened in disapproval. "A bad egg, that one."

"Well, according to Bruce he's here in Gotham now—dressed up like a card-carrying ninja warrior and trying to single-handedly take down Wayne Enterprises."

"Really?" Alfred looked startled. "That *is* distressing."

Dick leaned up against the table, his fingers tapping on the underside of the wooden rim. "I think Bruce is seriously worried that he can't take this guy. He won't admit it, of course. . . ."

"He *never* admits fear, Master Dick. Surely you've learned that by now." Alfred added the last utensil to the pile. At the same moment he and Dick became aware that they were no longer alone in the kitchen. They turned to see Bruce standing in the doorway, dressed in a tuxedo.

"Master Bruce," Alfred said. "I—that is, we—"

Bruce lifted his hand. "I have a charity function to attend at the museum this evening. I should be back by midnight." He turned and left the room.

Dick clicked his tongue against his teeth. "Do you think he heard us?"

Alfred gave a sigh and began to gather up the spotless silverware. "Who can tell?" he said.

Light sparkled from the high windows of the Gotham Natural History Museum, while tantalizing strains of classical music drifted out into the walled parking lot where expensive cars gleamed in precise rows. Many of them were limousines. With a faint whisper of noise, a black-clad figure descended on a rope down the wall of the museum and disappeared among the automobiles.

In the hallway outside the reception room, Summer Gleeson scowled at a pair of muscular museum guards, tapping her foot impatiently as she looked from one impassive face to the other.

"Look, Tiny." She addressed her remarks to the smaller of the two behemoths. "I'm with the *press, capice*? Television?" She sketched a large rectangle in the air in front of his face. "Or don't they have cable in the cave where you live?"

"I'm sorry, Ms. Gleeson." His voice was a pleasant baritone, and struck her as being very well modulated for someone who so closely resembled a bulldog in uniform. "No invite, no entry."

Summer fumed, turning her attention to the other giant. "You and Godzilla here are just lucky I don't have my cameraman with me. I'd have your face all over the evening news!"

"Gee." The second guard allowed himself an ingenuous grin. "My dear old mom would be so proud!"

Summer shook her head in disgust and turned her back on the two men. She had never been particularly fond of Neanderthals, no matter how they were dressed.

Above the posh reception room, a crystal chandelier reflected light from a thousand facets. A snow-white banner hung over the center of the room, proclaiming:

WAYNE CHARITIES RECEPTION

The music of Tchaikovsky played discreetly over the public address system as men and women in formal evening wear chatted, gossiped, and consumed large quantities of hors d'oeuvres and champagne.

Bruce Wayne stood at the edge of the crowd, sipping at his glass of sparkling water with an air of slight distraction. He exchanged small talk with the occasional guest who wandered by, looking trapped when he suddenly became the center of attention of a roving group of about a dozen representatives of Gotham's upper crust. He waited for an opening and politely excused himself, heading immediately for the exit. He nodded to the matching linebackers at the door and started down the long hallway.

Summer Gleeson was lurking in a darkened doorway several yards down the corridor. She waited until Bruce passed, then slipped out and moved quietly down the hall behind him.

Bruce walked slowly, his eyes on the intricate labyrinth woven into the oriental carpet. He looked up as he neared a glassed-in exhibit of medieval Japanese armor and weaponry. His pace slowed to a stop. Summer flattened herself against the wall behind a life-size recreation of a parasaurolophus and watched him as he stood gazing at the display, his thoughts obviously somewhere else. . . .

It was a night in early spring. The dojo was dark and empty. As always, Master Yoru's longsword rested on the teakwood rack in its place of honor. Crickets sang in muted chorus through an open window.

A shadowy figure stole into the darkened room, moving directly to the longsword on its wooden stand. Black-gloved hands lifted the *daito* from the rack.

Light suddenly flooded the room. The thief whirled around.

Bruce stood in the doorway wearing his white combat trousers. His bare chest shone with sweat. He stepped into the room.

"Good thing I decided to practice tonight," he said in Japanese. His face and voice were both expressionless. "Yoru *Sensei* would grieve to lose that blade." His eyes traveled the length of the ornate scabbard. "It's over five hundred years old."

"True. And worth a fortune from the right collector of antiquities." Kyodai Ken nodded reasonably, his own voice carefully devoid of inflection. He studied the sword, then released it from his hands with a small sneer. Sheath and blade clattered to the floor. "But I have no need of a weapon to take care of you, Wayne-san."

The two men had started an unconscious circling dance, each maneuvering for the best location. Then Kyodai leaped at Bruce. The two fought in a whirlwind of blows and kicks, Kyodai slowly gaining the upper hand.

"Stop!" cried a commanding voice. Bruce and Kyodai sprang apart as if splashed with icy water.

Master Yoru walked from the doorway to stand before his countryman. His voice was calm, though his diminutive frame seemed to quiver with suppressed energy.

"You have dishonored the dojo, Kyodai," Yoru said softly. "You no longer have a place here." He lowered his eyes from the other man's face. "Go."

Kyodai's hands trembled. His contorted features were a study in anger and frustration beneath his shaven skull. He turned to glare at Bruce.

"You will pay for this, rich man's son! I will take all that you hold dear—and then I will *destroy* you!" He spat the words at his opponent, his voice lingering with a hiss on the word "destroy," until it sounded like the threat of an enraged serpent.

9

Bruce gave his head a melancholy shake and stepped back from the armor and weaponry exhibit. He turned and continued down the corridor, hands thrust in his pockets. Summer waited for a few heartbeats, then slipped from behind the bronze dinosaur and followed.

Bruce emerged from the building into the shadowed parking lot. There was a mild breeze, which brought with it a hint of welcome coolness and invested the sluggish air with the fresh scents of early summer. A uniformed attendant snapped to attention and hurried to fetch Bruce's car. Thirty seconds later, a low-slung, midnight blue convertible with the top up purred to a stop in front of him. The attendant hopped out, leaving the motor running and the driver's side door open. Bruce thanked him absentmindedly, pressing a tip into his palm as he got into the car.

Before he could swing his own door shut, the passenger door clicked open and Summer Gleeson flung herself into the other seat, a look of determined triumph on her attractive face.

Bruce glanced over at her.

"Why have you been following me all evening?" he asked calmly.

"You *knew*? How—" Summer sat back in surprise. "Never mind. Look—I know you don't like me very much, but I have a job to do."

Bruce rolled his eyes heavenward. "It's *late*, Ms. Gleeson—"

"I've done some research, Mr. Wayne." Summer leaned toward him intently. "I know you spent several years living in Japan when you were younger. Do you think the appearance of this ninja person here in Gotham City has anything to do with that? Is he trying to settle some sort of personal score by targeting your business holdings? Concerned Gothamites have a right to know why there's a new—and potentially very dangerous—nut case at large in their city."

At that moment the attendant moved closer to the driver's side of the car. He pushed Bruce's door shut and leaned down to the half-open window. "Have a nice trip, Mr. Wayne."

Bruce looked up in startlement at the sound of the harsh voice. There was a sharp hissing sound. A purple vapor began to stream up from beneath the seat as Kyodai Ken's smile drew back through a thickening haze. Bruce slumped forward.

The Japanese man drew a filter mask from his jacket and clapped it over his nose and mouth with one hand. He opened the door and shoved Bruce next to an equally immobilized Summer

Gleeson, then slid into the car. His hand reached for the gear shift and his foot found the gas pedal. Wisps of purple vapor trailed from the open driver's window as Kyodai Ken drove off into the darkness with his unconscious captives.

10

awn would soon be breaking in the outside world.

Leathery wings created a soft, constant sighing noise as a steady stream of errant tenants abandoned the search for food and returned to their perches in the high reaches of the Batcave. Far below, Dick Grayson stood under a cone of pale white light and buckled his golden utility belt into place around his narrow waist.

"Do you really think this is the proper thing to do, Master Dick?" Alfred stood just outside the lighted circle, a doubtful expression on his shadowed face. He was holding a silver tray on which rested a twisted strip of dark material. "You know how this sort of thing annoys him."

A green-gloved hand descended on the tray.

"Bruce is hours overdue from that charity thing, Alfred," Robin said, settling the black mask across his cheekbones. "We both know that's not like him."

The young man left the lighted area and mounted the branching ramp which connected it with a series of platforms on various levels. Lights came on over his head, glowing gradually brighter as he walked toward the Batcycle. He flipped switches on the control panel recessed into the body of the glossy black machine. Tiny lights flashed, and servos came on-line with a whine of power. The machine and the man turned together as the platform rotated slowly clockwise, aligning itself with the larger ramp that led toward the black mouth of the tunnel.

Robin checked the cycle's systems as Alfred stood by.

"There's a tracker in his car. . . ." A tiny screen displaying a map of Gotham City blinked on in the center of the control panel. A grid of black lines was superimposed on the map. Robin touched a button, and a tiny red dot pulsed in one corner with a steady beeping sound. "There he is now. At least that means the convertible's in one piece." The young man flashed Alfred a reassuring smile. "Maybe it's nothing. But I'll feel better once I've checked it out." He lifted the black helmet and lowered it onto his head. Then he gunned the engine. The Batcycle roared up the ramp and into the darkness.

The building was in an industrial area on the Gotham City docks, a low rambling structure whose brickwork was lost under a cloak of tenacious ivy. Beneath its dark windows, the surf pushed and pulled at barnacled pilings with the regular sound of a sleeper's breathing. A dilapidated wooden water tower stood in the center of the building's roof. A large sign mounted on its side read:

WAYNE ENTERPRISES
STORAGE

Inside, the warehouse was a repository for shadows and expensive objects. It took Bruce Wayne several bleary seconds after he regained consciousness to recognize his own property in the pale shafts of moonlight from the tall windows. Here were stored many of those possessions he had inherited or otherwise acquired over the years and which had not found a home elsewhere. He blinked slowly, his eyes scanning forests of statuary, foothills of furniture, islands of exotic items from around the world. Wooden crates, many of them still unopened, mounted toward the unseen ceiling, while high ropes divided the heavens with hanging tapestries.

Bruce craned his neck to see over the mound of objects directly in front of him and stifled a groan. His head ached. When he tried to move his body, he discovered without surprise that his hands and feet were securely bound. He was lying next to an unconscious Summer Gleeson on a pile of intricately figured Persian carpets.

A whisper of sound made him twist to look back over his shoulder. His head pounded.

The ninja stood there, motionless as a figure carved from obsidian. "Ah," said Kyodai Ken, "the rich man awakens." He tugged the hood and mask from his head, rubbed his palm over his hairless scalp. A close-trimmed beard and mustache now covered the lower portion of his face. "Remember me, rich man?"

Bruce was forced to keep his neck straining at

an unnatural angle in order to see the other man. "Yes," he said quietly, turning his face back into the shadows. "I remember you, Kyodai."

The Ninja reached out and prodded Bruce in the small of the back with his black-shod foot. "Kyodai-*san*, if you please, rich man. Your lack of respect dishonors us both." He moved a few steps to the right, bringing himself into Bruce's field of vision. "Indeed," he continued, "you should have little difficulty recalling the face of the man whose life you ruined. I was forced to become a thief after your meddling caused me to be cast out of the dojo."

Bruce grunted, moving slightly to ease the pressure of the ropes on his arms. "As I remember it, Kyodai, being a thief was what got you cast out in the first place."

The Ninja clucked his tongue in disapproval, lifting his eyes to scan the vast, treasure-filled darkness.

"Your wealth will be of much use to me. Do you have any idea how much those engraved *shuriken* cost? Of course, *you* never had to worry about money, did you, rich man? A parasite on the flesh of society, feeding on the blood and sweat of others. Flabby, soft, weak . . ." His dark eyes studied the bound form beneath him. "The game grows boring. It was too easy to defeat you."

There was a small moan from Bruce's side. Summer stirred and opened her eyes. She squinted into the shadows in confusion, her eyes widening when she recognized Bruce's face. "Where—where are we?"

The Ninja spared her a contemptuous glance, then returned his attention to Bruce. "I've stolen your secret bank codes at each theft. Soon I will have them all. After you are gone, I shall transfer the bulk of your money to my own private account."

"Wait. I don't get it. . . ." Summer had been listening dazedly to the Ninja's rhetoric. "You mean you're nothing but a common thief?"

Kyodai bristled. "Not a 'common' thief, woman." He gave a bark of forced laughter. "An *exceptional* thief. The very best. And since I have recently added kidnapping to my repertoire, you would do well to hold your tongue." He pulled his sword from its hidden sheath and moved to tower over Bruce. "And now, I fear, the game is drawing to its inevitable conclusion—"

An alarm bell began to jangle in the darkness. The Ninja froze. Reaching into the folds of his black garments, he drew forth a small device shaped like a television remote. He pressed a button on its side and the alarm stopped abruptly.

"It appears we have an unexpected guest." Kyodai bowed politely to his two captives. "This should not take long. Please amuse yourselves until my return." He sheathed his sword and pulled his mask and hood back into place before fading into the shadows.

Robin had parked the Batcycle next to Bruce's midnight blue sports car on the dock outside the warehouse. He spent ten minutes prowling around the outside of the building, investigating the possible entrances. As he stepped inside a

seemingly unguarded doorway, his ankle crossed a
thin electronic beam. An alarm went off inside the
warehouse as the circuit was broken. "Way to go,
Dick," Robin muttered to himself in disgust.
"Master crime fighter scores again."

He moved warily into the warehouse's labyrin-
thine interior, down the shadowed corridors
formed by stacked crates.

Robin's eyes adjusted slowly to the near-black-
ness. He had wandered through several crowded
storerooms when he heard a creak of wood from
somewhere above him. A black figure dropped
down in front of him like a spider ready to seize its
prey.

"Isn't it past your bedtime, small boy?" The
Ninja shifted his weight from foot to foot in a
slow, barely perceptible dance.

"Let's just see who ends up in slumberland in
the next couple of minutes," Robin said through
clenched teeth. He crouched in a fighting stance.

"Hai!" The Ninja was a blur of shadows. He
leaped at the younger man, the first two fingers on
his right hand pointed stiffly at his foe's throat.
Robin sidestepped the initial attack, managing to
parry the blow so that it sailed harmlessly by his
face. The Ninja darted past him and spun away.

Robin whirled toward his attacker, launching a
spinning back kick at the Ninja's head. Kyodai
stepped away easily, leaning back to allow Robin's
foot to fall well short of its target. "This is not a
movie show, small boy," he hissed. "Your blows
will have to connect in order to do any damage."
The two began to circle each other warily. Robin
noticed a small open window above a stack of

cardboard boxes. A portion of rusted metal railing was visible through the opening.

The Ninja seemed impatient. "Enough of this," he said after a few moments. "I have no time to coddle children. There is business I must attend to."

"Sure," Robin said with a smirk. "Not to mention the sore throat you must have developed from all the speechmaking you've—"

At that moment the Ninja was upon him. Robin felt the breeze from the warrior's blow as it swept millimeters from his throat. He ducked backward, stumbled against a crate, and launched himself into a back flip, praying that his aim was accurate enough in the shadowed room to get him where he wanted to go. He landed unsteadily on top of the stack of boxes, gauged the distance to the window, and shot through it like a swallow deserting a burning barn loft. His gloved hand closed on the railing and he swung himself swiftly around and up the ancient ladder. He pulled himself onto the moonlit rooftop with a sigh of relief.

He heard a snarl of rage from below. Seconds later the Ninja pulled himself up over the edge and confronted him.

"You try my patience, small boy!"

Robin edged backward past the rickety water tower as the black-clad warrior advanced on him with sword drawn. "Really? Well, heck—let's try some of mine, instead." He grinned at his older opponent. "You know, change of pace and all that."

As Robin was casting around for the best place to make his stand, the Ninja suddenly bounded forward in one of his astonishing leaps. Robin stepped to the side, puzzled as the other man landed several feet away, his sword striking the wood of one of the tower's legs with a resounding *chunk*.

"Hey, I'm over here," Robin chided, circling to keep the tower between them. "You didn't lose a contact lens in the middle of that last hop, by any chance?" He realized his mistake as he watched the Ninja set his palm against the weakened leg and heard the creak of wood.

The damaged strut gave way. The tower seemed to topple forward in slow motion. Halfway to the rooftop, it came apart at the seams. To Robin it seemed as if a dam had burst in the middle of the sky.

A large bronze statue of Ares, the Greek god of war, stood near the pile of carpets on which Bruce and Summer lay. One of Wayne Enterprises' subsidiaries had obtained it as partial payment for the debt incurred when a Greek shipping magnate with a penchant for gambling defaulted on the purchase of a luxury yacht. The god held a shield in one heavily muscled arm and a sharp-edged sword in the other. Bruce forced himself to wait a full thirty seconds after Kyodai's departure, then he began to inch his way like a caterpillar toward the statue.

Summer watched him anxiously. "What are you doing?"

"Quiet!" Bruce whispered sharply. Backing up until he was seated precariously on a rolled-up carpet next to the statue, he began to saw the ropes binding his hands against the bottom edge of the god's sword.

Minutes passed and Summer's attention wandered as Bruce worked steadily to cut through his bonds.

"Look what I discovered among the rich man's spoils."

Summer gave a gasp of surprise as the Ninja stepped out of the shadows. A water-soaked figure clad in dark green and red was slung carelessly over his shoulder. Kyodai leaned down and dropped Robin onto a nearby pile of carpets. The young man rolled into a sitting position and surveyed his fellow captives.

"Summer Gleeson, of *Inside Gotham* fame. Bruce Wayne, noted businessman and philanthropist." Robin nodded pleasantly to the other two. "Fancy meeting you here." He was also bound, hand and foot, with thin black cord. Water dripped steadily from the end of his nose.

"Inform me if the child grows tiresome," the Ninja said. Turning his back, he began to remove his hood and mask. "Not having had the luxury of a recent dousing myself," he commented, "I must make myself more comfortable in this miserable swelter." Kyodai peeled off his black shirt, revealing the tattooed dragon in all its coiled complexity. A small noise made him turn back to his captives. He raised an eyebrow.

Bruce was standing at the edge of the piled carpets, massaging his wrists. A length of frayed black cord lay at his feet.

"Oh, really?" the Ninja said, as he smiled and settled into a fighting crouch. "The rich man requests another beating. Fortunately, I am a generous soul."

The quiet man in evening dress and the shirtless ninja began to circle each other in the crowded darkness. Robin watched the combatants closely, noting Bruce's quick glance at Summer Gleeson. He understood the concern behind the look immediately, and began to scan the piles of exotic objects for a way to help his partner. His eyes fell on a length of stout rope anchored to a hook set in the floor a few feet from him, then followed it to a huge tapestry hanging rolled up just below the ceiling.

Kyodai stepped in with a python's speed. He grabbed Bruce and hurled him through the air. Bruce smacked into a pile of woven baskets, sending them scattering with the impact as he thrashed on the floor. The Ninja sneered at his struggling foe, hands on hips. "You have lost all your skill, Wayne!" he crowed. "Even a white belt could have avoided that throw."

Summer shook her head as Bruce climbed slowly to his feet. "Stop it! Can't you see he's no match for you?"

"But that's the joke, woman." The Ninja advanced in a slow, creeping fashion, his legs splayed. "He never was!" He lowered his head for an instant, then leaped into the air. "*Hai!*"

Kyodai slammed a side kick into Bruce's midsection, knocking the other man back into the clutter of baskets. Bruce groaned with the impact and pulled himself shakily to his feet.

Robin inched with torturous slowness toward the hook in the floor. "Hang in there, Bruce," he murmured softly, scooting the last few inches across the wooden boards. The statue of Ares stood not far away.

The Ninja's next attack sent Bruce crashing into a pile of bamboo bird cages.

"Tired yet, Wayne? I haven't even broken a sweat." The black-clad warrior's haughty grin turned into a snarl. *"Get up."*

Bruce clambered stiffly to his feet. Perspiration dripped from his face, and his hair and clothing were covered with bits of shattered bamboo. Kyodai sank into his fighting stance again, twirling his hands through an intricate series of circle blocks across his body. He ended up crouching forward, his hands open and his fingers arched like claws.

Summer winced as Bruce shambled painfully toward the other man. The Ninja gave a theatrical sigh. "Well, I have had enough exercise for one night," he said. Then his voice grew hard: "Now it *ends,* rich man."

Measuring the angle carefully in the dimness, Robin cocked his leg and kicked at the statue. The god fell in a slow arc, his upraised sword biting deeply into the thick rope. There was a groan from up near the ceiling, followed by a moment's silence. Then the last strands of rope parted and the heavy tapestry unrolled, falling to hang like a curtain between Summer Gleeson and the two combatants. Dust motes swam in the silver moonlight.

"Hey!" Summer blinked in surprise.

As Bruce watched the tapestry unroll, the posture of his body shifted smoothly from a tottering

crouch into a compact fighting stance. Robin
grinned from his new vantage point in the shadows. "All *right*!" he exulted under his breath.
"New sheriff in town!"

Kyodai's eyes narrowed as he took in his opponent's sudden recovery. He paused for a micro-
second, then leaped at the other man.

Bruce changed positions easily, grabbing the
Ninja's arm and tossing him high. Robin's grin
grew wider when he saw the black-clad warrior
sail through the air. *"Yes!"*

Behind the dusty tapestry, Summer Gleeson
bit her lower lip at the crash of impact, fearing the
worst as she imagined an already-battered Bruce
Wayne meeting defeat at the deadly hands of their
assailant.

On the other side of the curtain, it was Kyodai
who sprawled in the shattered remnants of a crate
of porcelain vases. He looked up, astonished.

Bruce stood facing him with one hand extended, the forefinger curling in a summoning
gesture. "Come here," he said in a quiet voice.

The Ninja pulled himself erect, crouched, and
began to circle.

"Gotten a second wind, have you? Or perhaps
you've grown a new backbone. Good—the game
regains its spark. This will make your destruction
all the more satisfying."

Bruce shifted to a high-aikido stance, watching the Ninja with an almost imperious gaze. He
waved his hands in a complex display of inward
and upward snake blocks, halting in a cat stance:
palms open, one hand high, one low. "Shut up
and fight," he said softly.

"Hai!" The Ninja exploded in a furious charge. Bruce centered his attention on the body hurtling toward him, readying himself to execute the same series of moves he had employed against Dick in the gym at Wayne Manor. When Kyodai closed with him, it was as if the Japanese warrior had hurtled into the blade of a high-speed buzz saw. The Ninja's body was launched twisting and flailing into a collection of abstract paintings. He fell heavily to the floor among the ruined canvases. Bruce surveyed the damage with a mental shrug. Luckily the artist had not been one of his favorites.

"You are no man," the Ninja rasped, getting unsteadily to his feet. His face showed his amazement. "You are a demon!"

Bruce took a step forward. "You were right about one thing, Kyodai," he said in a low, husky voice. "Now it ends."

The Ninja backed away, his face dark with fear. Turning, he snatched up the carved head of an eighteenth dynasty Egyptian scribe and zigzagged through the piles of objects toward a boarded-up window. He hurled the stone carving ahead of him, smashing a ragged hole through a section of the wooden planks. Then he dived after it, twisting in midair to crash feetfirst through the remaining boards. An instant later a loud splash sounded from below.

When Bruce reached the window, ripples were still spreading outward through the dark water. His adversary was nowhere to be seen.

11

An hour later, the reddish glow of dawn filled the library at Wayne Manor, as Bruce and Dick relaxed over an impromptu breakfast served on spindle-legged, red and black lacquered Japanese trays. With twenty minutes notice, Alfred had provided the weary duo with eggs Benedict, hash brown potatoes, and slices of chilled cantaloupe garnished with strawberries. Now the butler stood by the window in pajamas and robe and surveyed the nearly empty plates with quiet satisfaction.

"Weather report says the heat's broken. Next few days should be cool and dry." Dick folded the morning paper and took a long, thirsty swig of fresh-squeezed grapefruit juice. He glanced at Bruce, who seemed lost in thought. "So what did you end up telling Summer?"

"The truth." Bruce set down his fork and pushed his plate away. "That Batman arrived after the tapestry unrolled and took care of the Ninja." He tilted a silver creamer filled with nonfat milk over his steaming coffee cup.

"That's the way it happened, all right." Dick's

grin was fleeting. "The police recovered the stone head he tossed out the window," he said to Alfred, "but they couldn't find any trace of Kyodai Ken." He turned back to Bruce. "You think he escaped?"

"Probably." Bruce took a sip of decaf, set down his cup, and sat with fingers tented in front of his face. "Ninja are very resourceful—this one in particular."

"Speaking of matters Japanese . . ." Dick raised an eyebrow at Alfred. "When are you finally gonna break down and teach me how to play this go game?" He winked at Bruce and glanced at his wristwatch. "I've got a little free time right now, as a matter of fact. Just give me a quick rundown of the rules and I'll beat you a couple of matches."

"Do forgive me for putting you off for so long," Alfred said drily. The butler left the window and went to the far wall. He pushed a wheeled ladder several yards from its resting place and climbed up to pull a slim volume from the topmost shelf. Then he carried the book to the couch and handed it to Dick. "I suggest you study this carefully before we attempt our first game, Master Dick. The rules are deceptively simple, the strategy extremely sophisticated."

"Hmm. *The Beginner's Guide to Go,*" Dick read from the cover. "Cool." He took the book from Alfred and leaned back into the couch.

The butler lingered by Bruce's chair, stacking dishes and loading them onto a silver tray. He cleared his throat after a moment. "Do you think he might return, Master Bruce?"

"It doesn't matter." Bruce shrugged. "I defeated him once. If necessary, I can do it again."

Dick looked up from the book with a skeptical expression. "Oh, sure." He waved his palm in an offhand gesture. "Like rolling off a log, wasn't it? *No problemo* at all." He shook his head at the older man. "Come clean, Bruce. Deep down inside, weren't you maybe the slightest bit worried —for a second or two?"

"I wasn't worried. Still . . ." Bruce paused, took a deep breath. "Thanks for your help. It would have been harder to find a way to beat him with Summer watching." He got to his feet and moved toward the window. "Maybe even impossible," he said quietly over his shoulder.

Dick exchanged a startled glance with Alfred over the pages of the go manual. As compliments went, it wasn't exactly a testimonial—but it was a great deal more than he'd expected.

Bruce Wayne stood at the window with his hands clasped behind his back and contemplated the rising sun.

12

onths passed, and summer came and went in Gotham City. Autumn arrived with an early cold snap, as the air turned crisp and leaves flashed suddenly scarlet.

Alfred Pennyworth was standing in front of the large oven in the kitchen of Wayne Manor, a blue gingham pot holder in one hand and an oven mitt shaped like a killer whale in the other, when the sonorous chimes of the front doorbell brought a furrow of displeasure to his patrician brow. He watched as the red second hand on the wall clock continued its slow, steady progress around the dial. Just two more minutes . . .

The doorbell rang again. A sigh escaped Alfred's lips as he removed the mitt and placed it on the butcher block table next to the pot holder. As he turned to leave the kitchen, the butler fixed the oven door with a commanding stare. "Do *not* fall," he ordered the soufflé that waited behind the shiny surface.

There was a feather duster hanging just inside the kitchen doorway. Alfred plucked it from its hook as he passed through the swinging door. As he made his way down the long hallway to the front of the house, he scanned the pieces of furniture and artwork that lined the corridor, reaching out automatically with the duster to touch up those surfaces that had begun to lose their shine. He paused briefly to neaten the small piles of mail that sat on the Chippendale credenza beside the front door, making sure that the latest colorful postcard from Master Dick's circus tour was prominently displayed on top. Then he set down the duster and grasped the polished door handle.

The person who stood on the doorstep was about Alfred's height, though considerably larger in girth. The bulky torso was clothed in a faded blue silk dress under a brown cloth coat that had seen better days. An orange pillbox hat with a short black veil perched at a ridiculous angle on a mass of blonde curls that were obviously the result of a dye job of dubious quality. Lavender high heels and a red and green plaid scarf completed the unusual ensemble. Behind the dark veil, the coarse features were the unhealthy color of putty.

"Yes?" Alfred inclined his head, his mind on the delicate creation already beginning to languish in the oven. "May I help you . . . madam?"

"Why, yes—" The voice was surprisingly thick and rasping. The newcomer broke off and tried again after a round of throat clearing. "I mean, why, I hope so, young man." This time the words emerged in quavering, high-pitched tones from the scarlet lips. "I'm supposed to be meeting my niece and I'm afraid I've lost my way." The visitor peered around the edge of the door, veiled eyes sweeping the ornate foyer behind the butler. "Such a lovely house you have!"

"And who might your niece be?" Alfred inquired, keeping a firm hand on the edge of the heavy door.

"Oh, well," the person behind the veil quavered. "She's actually somewhere in this neighborhood visiting her fiancé. You'll think me awfully foolish, but I can't recall his name." Heavily veined and wrinkled hands pawed at a small black purse. "I do have his number in here, though, so if you'd just allow me to use your tele —tele—" The rasping edge returned to the voice as the blonde head turned and a plump finger slipped up beneath the veil. "Sorry. I seem to have caught a touch of the flu and I've been sneezing all morning. Now, if you'll just let me use your phone—" A fleshy arm came up to rest against the door and pushed forward with surprising strength. Alfred took a step backward, then held his ground. "If you would be so kind as to give me the number—" he began.

"I said, let me *in*!" The voice slipped to a rasping growl again as the stout figure pressed against the door with alarming force.

"Here, here—is there a problem now?"

Alfred raised his eyes to see a tall, blue-clad figure crossing the lawn toward the front steps. Sunlight glinted from the officer's silver badge.

"Gah!" The bulky visitor swiveled on the doorstep, eyes bulging beneath the veil. "I mean, good day to you, young man. I've decided not to make that call just now. I'm not feeling at all well." The ungainly figure leapt from the doorstep and hobbled with surprising speed along the side of the house in the opposite direction from the approaching policeman. It ducked into the bushes at the corner of the mansion and disappeared. A second later, Alfred heard a thunderous sneeze, followed by a peculiar noise similar to that made through a straw at the bottom of a milkshake, and a string of muttered imprecations that struck him as decidedly unladylike.

"Afternoon, sir. Lovely day. Were you havin' a bit of a set-to with the lady, then?" The officer was a large, barrel-chested man with thick red hair and a slight lilt to his speech. A small scar led from beneath his left eye to the bottom of his ruddy cheek.

"I am almost certain that was no lady." Alfred squinted at the bushes, his expression thoughtful. "And at any rate, our only disagreement involved the use of the telephone."

"Ah, well, lady or not, I didn't like the looks of her." The big man frowned suspiciously at the corner of the mansion. "Probably won't hurt t' radio in a description t' the station house." He stepped away from the door, then turned back, face apologetic. "Ah, y'wouldn't mind if *I* was t' come in an' make use of your phone, would you, sir? The radio in my squad car's been actin' up all day. I think it's sunspots."

"Not at all." Alfred stepped to one side and ushered the large man into the foyer. "Oh, by the way, I found your last missive most amusing," he said as he led the way past the small table. "Do remind me to show it to Master Bruce when he returns home from his meeting with Mr. Fox."

"My, uh—what?" The policeman reached up to scratch beneath his cap. His broad cheeks had flushed a deeper shade of red. "Uh, did you say—"

"Your postcard, Master Dick." Alfred paused to tap the brightly colored rectangle on the table-top. "Now come along, and we'll get you that telephone as soon as I've rescued my cheese souf-flé."

The man in blue stopped short, as if he had suddenly walked into a wall of glass in the hallway. He blew air out through his cheeks and shook his head. *"How,* Alfred? Just tell me *how."* The lilt had left his voice, which now sounded like that of a much younger man. "I've studied with one of the world's great masters of disguise, I've prac-ticed and practiced, yet you always . . ." His voice trailed off and he stood shaking his head mournfully at the polished floor. Then he raised his eyes. "Soufflé, huh? Got any hot chocolate to go with it?"

"Certainly, Master Dick. If you would care to remove your . . . things, I'll brew some up at once. My word—is that *clay* you're tracking all over the floor? How on earth did your shoes get so dirty?"

"Search me. They were clean when I put 'em on." Dick Grayson removed the gray-streaked black shoes, opened the door, and set them care-fully just outside. Stepping back from the en-tranceway, the ersatz officer took off his blue cap, his red wig, and the scar beneath his left eye. As Dick began to peel away the remaining layers of his costume, Alfred leaned his head out through the doorway and gave the bushes a final perusal, his forehead creased in puzzlement.

"You know, there was something quite familiar about that curious individual, despite an absolutely ghastly fashion sense." He dismissed the puzzle with a shrug. "I simply cannot place the face. . . ."

The brown-haired man with the sad face had kept the motor running while he waited in a cul-de-sac not far from the winding road that led up to Wayne Manor. He tapped nervously on the steering wheel, looking up from the bodybuilder's magazine he was reading to scan the road for patrolling police cars. He started when a low hedge of bushes began to rustle near the car. Then the handle clicked on the right rear door and the door swung slowly outward.

The driver gulped silently and clenched his jaw, watching the rearview mirror with an unwilling fascination as something large and grayish half climbed, half flowed into the backseat. The hairs prickled at the back of his neck. All this time, he thought, and he still hadn't gotten used to it.

He focused his gaze on the dashboard while his passenger composed himself, wincing at the sucking, slurping sounds that issued from the back of the vehicle.

"How'd it go?" he asked finally.

"It didn't." The voice was thick and guttural. "Some nosy copper showed up when I was almost inside. I think my hunch was right—they prob'ly patrol this whole area day and night. We better find ourselves a less exclusive neighborhood if I'm

gonna score some quick cash for my treatments."
The thing in the back seat gave a series of moist,
racking coughs. "I coulda taken the cop and the
skinny butler both, if I was in better shape. But
this flu's got me all messed up. Anyway, I started
to feel a big sneeze comin' on, and figgered I better hightail it outta there. You know what happens
when I sneeze. . . ."

"Yeah." The driver stuck a finger inside his
collar and tugged. It had begun to feel a bit warm
in the car.

"You know, I'm startin' to get that feelin' like
I'm not all here," the rasping voice continued. "I
think I might've left a little bit behind on the
doorstep." There was a quiet squishing sound of
the sort the driver had learned to associate with a
shrug. "Ah, who cares—it'll get back to me
sooner or later."

The driver repressed a shudder. "Why don't
we just head down ta the clinic and try ta con
somethin' offa Dr. Thompkins, like before? You
know you're not yourself since you came down
with this flu stuff. I told you not ta try anything
till you shake it off."

"Yeah, yeah, Teddy—you told me. Now shut
up and get us out of here."

"Sure thing." Teddy put the car into gear and
eased them out onto the main road. He glanced
up in the mirror and blanched. "Uh, Matt?" he
said tentatively. "I don't wanna upset you or
nothin', but your nose is upside down. . . ."

He looked away as the awful sounds began
again.

13

So, Master Dick . . ." Alfred brought two mugs of steaming cocoa to the butcher block table and seated himself on a high stool. "Was your summer migration with Haly's Big Top as rewarding as you had hoped it would be?"

"It was terrific, Alfred." Dick took a swig of the hot liquid and smacked his lips. "Getting the chance to hang out with Mr. Haly and Belle and all the rest of them—it was like I was visiting relatives, you know? They really were like an extended family to me, back when the Flying Graysons used to headline at the big top."

"Families can come in many different forms," Alfred agreed with a nod, tasting his own hot chocolate.

"Yeah." Dick leaned over with a napkin and dabbed a spot of chocolate milk from the older man's neatly trimmed mustache. "And I also got to polish up a lot of my acrobatic skills. You remember I told you about Ellie Mercer—the new lead flyer? She and I got to be a real team by the end of the tour. Oh, and something else—" He tilted back on his stool to reach behind him.

After changing into jeans and a T-shirt, Dick had retrieved his belongings from their place of concealment under a hedge at the edge of the Wayne estate. Now he lifted his backpack from the black-and-white tiled floor. He lowered it onto the table and opened the main compartment with a crackle of Velcro. "Look what I've got."

He brought out a rectangular parcel wrapped in a frayed square of red silk and placed it in front of the butler.

Alfred lifted back the cloth and removed a hinged box made of polished wood. "My word!" The box unfolded into a square board covered with a grid of intersecting black lines, while hidden in its interior were two small, covered wooden bowls, one made of rosewood and one of carved mulberry. Alfred set the bowls on the table and carefully opened their lids. The rosewood bowl was filled with a quantity of flat black stones; the pieces in the mulberry bowl were white. "Master Dick, this is one of the most beautiful go sets I have ever seen." He lifted one of the white stones and placed it on the board with a quick snapping sound. The butler smiled appreciatively. "Genuine shell," he commented, "and *kaya* wood for the board! It must be worth a small fortune. Wherever did you come across such a marvel?"

"It was a gift," Dick told him. "Remember in one of my letters I mentioned a guy they called Oakie, a roustabout who doubled as a clown now and then? Well, his full name is Akira Oki and he was born in Yokohama. We got to talking one evening and I mentioned that you were trying to

teach me something about go. He brightened
right up and got out this set. Turns out he used to
play the game for a living back in Japan. He said
his rank was professional nine dan. That's pretty
high, isn't it?"

"Pretty high? Professional nine dan is the
highest rank awarded." Alfred was quietly incred-
ulous. "Master Dick," he asked, "what on earth
was a nine dan go player doing working for Phin-
eas Haly's Big Top?"

Dick shrugged. "I think he was on some sort
of a sabbatical. He said he needed time off to ex-
plore other cultures and professions. He was interested in the high wire, too, so I traded him
some flying lessons for a go tutorial. At the end of
the summer he told me he wanted me to have
this. Wouldn't take no for an answer." Dick lifted
the rosewood bowl and poured some of the black
stones into his palm. "He was pretty good at
clown makeup, too." He passed the mulberry
bowl to Alfred and centered the board between
them on the table. "Want to play?"

When Bruce arrived home from a day of business
meetings at Wayne Enterprises' corporate headquarters, he was surprised to find that dinner was
not prepared and waiting for him for the first time
in his memory. Instead, Alfred and Dick sat
hunched over the go board at the kitchen table,
their attention riveted on the pattern of black and
white stones that covered a third of the board.
Alfred glanced up at the wall clock as his employer
entered the room.

"Heavens, how did it become so late?" The

elderly butler left his stool and began making hurried preparations for dinner while Bruce greeted Dick with a clap on the shoulder and a tousle of the younger man's hair.

"It's a special occasion, Alfred," Dick said with a mischievous grin. "How about we just send out for pizza?"

The expression on Alfred's face sent the two chuckling into the living room, where Bruce sprawled on one of the big couches while Dick paced in front of him, relating his summertime adventures traveling with the big top.

"I've never seen Mr. Haly happier, Bruce. This grant program of yours was a great idea! Oh, he sent along a year-end report for the Wayne Foundation. It's with my stuff."

Bruce nodded. "I'm glad it's working out. By the way, I noticed some of your 'stuff' on my way in the door. Don't tell me your fascination with Japanese games is spilling over into other aspects of their culture. I've never known you to leave your shoes on the front step before."

"Oh, yeah, I forgot about them. The soles were full of mud, and Alfred was afraid I'd track it all over the house."

"Mud?" Bruce raised his brows. "They were perfectly clean when I picked them up. I left them in the foyer."

"That's weird. They were filthy when I put them out there. Which reminds me. The oddest-looking woman stopped by this—"

Alfred stuck his head in the living room at that moment and announced dinner. The two sus-

pended their conversation while they went to
wash up.

Over dinner Bruce told Dick that he had been
working on a few modifications to the Batmobile
during the summer. "I managed to come up with
a couple of interesting ideas," he said. "If you're
not too worn out on your first night home, we
can do a little patrolling later and I'll show you
what I did."

"All right!" Dick rubbed his hands together.
"Back in the saddle again. Do I get to drive?"

Two hours later, the pair stood in the Batcave in
front of the polished black vehicle.

"Doesn't look any different from the outside." Robin adjusted his mask and tilted his head
sideways at the futuristic machine. "What'd you
do, install a multiple CD player and soup up the
speakers?" He struck an imaginary chord on the
air guitar. "We can serenade the crooks before we
bag 'em."

"The alterations we came up with were a bit
more practical," Batman told him. "Though
'bagging them' isn't that far off the mark." He
walked to the far side of the Batmobile and
climbed into the cockpit. "Now, are you going to
stand there or are you going to drive?"

"Really?" Robin trotted to the driver's side
and vaulted into the seat. "Psyched!"

"It makes sense for you to practice now and
then," Batman commented as his young partner
started the engine. "You never know when you
might need to operate the vehicle—in an emer-
gency, that is."

"Yeah, yeah, I get it." Robin revved the motor while the big turntable rotated slowly, bringing the nose of the Batmobile into alignment with the exit ramp. "Don't get too used to this seat, right?" He hit the accelerator and the car blazed up the ramp on its tail of fire.

"So when do I get to see the new additions?" Robin asked as he guided the Batmobile along the winding back road that would bring it to Gotham City.

"We'll play it by ear," Batman told him. "If we don't have an opportunity to put them to use, we can find a deserted area and I'll demonstrate."

They rode in silence for a while. "So, I've told you all about my summer," Robin said as the city loomed before them, a man-made mountain range carved out of darkness and spangled with webs of light. "How was yours?"

"Things came up. I dealt with them." Batman gave a shrug. "The time passed."

Robin nodded. "I did manage to follow some of it, what with the news and Alfred's letters. I gather our Ninja friend never surfaced again."

"No sign of him," said the Dark Knight. "If Kyodai did survive the river, he must have decided to do his drying out somewhere other than Gotham City."

"Good for him." Robin surveyed the glittering cityscape. "Gotham's got enough home-grown troublemakers. We don't have to import them. Alfred told me the Scarecrow busted out of Arkham again."

Batman nodded grimly. "Still at large. Riddler's back behind bars as of last month, however.

And I brought Harley and Ivy in a few days ago after another joyride. There were some minor skirmishes with organized crime, a hostage-taking and a holdup or two. No other major developments."

"Great. I'm glad it's been so quiet." Robin hesitated. "I heard about the big blowup down at the animal research center. The newscast made it sound like there was . . . um . . . 'feline involvement' in the disturbance." He glanced doubtfully at his partner. "Did you—"

"Keep your eyes on the road," Batman said shortly. He peered into the darkness outside the canopy. "I handled it. No formal charges were made."

"Good, that's good. Well, here we are." Robin turned the car onto one of the main thoroughfares as they entered the city. "The usual route?"

Gotham seemed relatively quiet as the crime fighters prowled the streets and alleyways. The mere presence of the Batmobile was enough to quell an altercation outside a bar, while drug dealers and their clients dispersed into the shadows at the futuristic vehicle's approach. They patrolled the city on an inwardly spiraling route, moving over the course of two hours from the more affluent sections of town to the seedy neighborhoods known collectively as Crime Alley.

They were halfway down Park Row when Robin noticed the light in the window of the free clinic. "Isn't it a little late—even for Dr. Leslie?" he asked. "Hey, it just went out."

"Pull over and park at the curb on the other

side of the alleyway," Batman instructed. "We might as well check it out."

Robin coasted the Batmobile to a stop. He twined his fingers together and cracked his knuckles. "Let me," he offered. "It's been too long!"

14

"Size up the situation quietly," Batman ordered. He slid over into the driver's seat while Robin exited the vehicle. "If there's something going on in there, don't try to handle it yourself. If you do get stuck, do your best to send them out to me."

"Yes, sir. Right, sir. Anything else, sir?" Robin gave an exaggerated salute as he left the side of the vehicle and prowled along the edge of the clinic, keeping low to the ground as he passed beneath the large storefront windows. He gave the doorknob a measured twist. It turned with a muffled click.

He eased the door open and slipped inside the darkened main room. There was always a chance Dr. Leslie Thompkins or one of her co-workers had decided to put in a few extra hours catching up on paperwork—but if that was the case, where had the light gone? He moved noiselessly across the old wooden floor, freezing in position when a floorboard creaked under his boot. He counted off thirty seconds and started off again. He was heading for the small cluster of examining rooms and offices that made up the back of the clinic. Chances were, the light he had seen had come from one of those.

As he started down the short corridor that connected the back rooms, a sound came from the farthest office, the one used by Dr. Thompkins herself. It sounded like a muffled sneeze. Robin held his breath, listening. Then he saw a thin strip of light suddenly appear beneath the door. He stepped lightly to the end of the corridor and grasped the handle. Then he counted to three and yanked the door wide.

"Oh, my goodness!" The elderly woman who sat behind the desk lifted a handkerchief to her mouth in startlement. The room was dimly lit by a small desk lamp. Robin relaxed as he saw Dr. Thompkins' familiar features at the edge of the circle of yellow light.

"Dr. Leslie—sorry I frightened you." Robin gestured to the dark hallway behind him. "I was driving by and I noticed the light. It was pretty late, so it seemed like a good idea to check it out."

"And a good thing you did, young man. One can never be too careful in a neighborhood like this." Her voice was muffled behind the handkerchief, and sounded huskier than he'd remembered. "You'll have to excuse me. I've got some dreadful allergy and my nose has been running like a garden hose." She gave a significant glance at the mounds of paper sprawling on the cluttered desk. "I'm trying to finish up these reports so I can go home and get some rest."

"Oh, sure, Dr. Leslie. Just wanted to make

sure everything was all right." As Robin turned to
leave the office, he noticed a small quantity of
grayish mud on the floor by the side of the desk.
He stopped with his hand on the doorknob. "Tell
you what," he said. "I'll just wait while you finish
up what you're doing. Then I'll give you a ride to
your apartment. It's really too late to be walking
the streets of Crime Alley by yourself."

"Oh." The figure on the other side of the
desk regarded him thoughtfully from behind the
handkerchief. She plucked a fragment of lint from
her brightly patterned purple and yellow shawl.
"How, uh, considerate of you." She opened the
top desk drawer and removed two brown plastic
pill bottles, which she dropped quickly into a
small black purse. "Medicine," she explained.
"For the allergy." Leaning back in her chair, she
lifted a metal letter opener in her slender hands.
"You did say that you were out patrolling by
yourself tonight, didn't you?" she asked, toying
with the silver dagger.

"That's right." Robin leaned against the
doorjamb with arms folded. "All by myself."

"Good, good." She suddenly let go of the letter opener, which dropped onto the desk with a
sharp noise. She picked it up and immediately released it again, producing a second rap. "Goodness, I'm all thumbs tonight!"

"Probably that allergy," Robin suggested. He
tensed his muscles slightly when he heard the faint
creak from the hallway at his back, keeping his
gaze fixed on the face of the room's other occupant. When her eyes flicked momentarily to a
place slightly above his left shoulder, Robin

feinted to the right, reached back, and tightened his hands on the upraised arm of the man standing directly behind him.

The man dropped his revolver as Robin flipped him over his shoulder and sent him flying through the air. The frail figure behind the desk ducked to one side as the attacker crashed against the far wall and dropped to the floor. "Sorry," Robin said. "Kind of a nervous tic I've developed when people try to knock me out without asking first."

"You miserable punk—" The elderly woman's voice was gone, replaced by a thick, guttural rasp. As Robin watched, the thing in the chair began to swell and contract, skin and clothing flowing together like a painting left out in the rain, until the colors and textures merged into a grayish-brown amorphous mass. A cavernous mouth yawned suddenly above a massive jaw, while tiny eyes blazed in the damp-looking brow. "Outta my way!" The creature reared back in the squeaking office chair, then launched itself at the doorway in a thick stream of liquefied matter.

Robin flattened himself against the wall of the corridor with distaste as gobbets of moist tissue splattered against his face and chest. There was a protracted sucking sound as the thing re-formed itself in the main room, then heavy footsteps pounded toward the front door.

"Yuck." Robin brushed the damp clods from his skin and clothing. They fell to the floor where they began to writhe sluggishly in the direction of the street. The young crime fighter paused long enough to snap a pair of lightweight handcuffs on the sad-faced man who lay groaning behind the desk. Then he took off after the fleeing creature.

Robin burst through the front door of the clinic, then stopped in his tracks. As the bloblike criminal lumbered toward the end of the block, the Batmobile suddenly pulled into view from a nearby alleyway. "Stop right there, Clayface!" ordered an amplified voice from inside the car.

The creature gave a howl of fury. It swung its right arm back, then hurled a thickened glob of its own substance toward the approaching vehicle. The mass of hardened protoplasm struck the front of the Batmobile like a cannonball. Robin winced.

A tiny flap snapped open on the hood of the black vehicle and a small nozzle protruded. As Robin looked on, a filmy cloud of flimsy-looking material sprayed from the nozzle in the direction of the shape-changing criminal. It enveloped the thing like a translucent parachute, tightening rapidly about the grayish hulk. As the captive creature struggled, cries of rage mingled with a noise like someone trying to pull his boot out of a swamp. In seconds the creature was immobilized, lying on the street wrapped in see-through material like a piece of steak in the supermarket.

"Not bad," Robin remarked to his partner as the Dark Knight left the Batmobile's cockpit and approached the captive monster. "I take it this is one of the little extras you put in."

"That's right." Batman looked down at the motionless creature with quiet satisfaction. "You've just witnessed its first field test. It's a superstrong polymer, porous enough to let air pass through it, but nothing else—not even something as malleable as our friend here."

They collected the other intruder from the back office after finding the real Leslie Thompkins bound and gagged in the adjoining room. "I hope you weren't taken in by that insulting attempt at mimicry," she told Robin sternly as she massaged her wrists. "The hair was abominable, and he didn't even come close to imitating my voice."

"Didn't buy it for a second, Dr. Leslie," Robin insisted, his hand making crossing motions above his heart. "Besides, Alfred's right—the guy's got lousy fashion sense."

15

With their evening's catch safely deposited in a special cell at Arkham Asylum, Batman and Robin returned to the Batcave. Alfred met them as they disembarked from the Batmobile, carrying a silver tray piled with assorted raw vegetables and a cup of yogurt dip. "No! No! Not that!" Robin shielded his eyes as he raced past the elderly butler and headed for the elevator. "It's nachos I want, with lots of thick, gooey cheese! Man the microwave!"

The next morning Bruce received an early call from Lucius Fox, his second in command at Wayne Enterprises. Fox had just been informed that the corporation's main Japanese subsidiary had been burglarized a few hours earlier.

"The MO's identical to that ninja character's who was causing us so much trouble over here a few months ago," Fox reported. "Could be a copycat—or even a coincidence, I suppose, but . . ."

"Doubtful," Bruce agreed. "I figured it was just a matter of time till he resurfaced." He thought for a moment. "I guess the best thing to do is let the authorities over there handle it. If the Ninja's back in action, I'm sure we'll hear more from him before too long. Anything else, Lucius?"

"Oh, lawyers for Daggett Development are threatening to file suit over that crooked takeover bid for Rainville Renewal we helped squash last year." Fox chuckled. "Doesn't seem like they'll have much credibility before a judge—considering their chief exec's behind bars at the moment. Should we get ready for a fight, just in case?"

"Nothing like senseless litigation to take your mind off your real problems." Bruce sighed into the phone. "Might as well get the legal department working on it. Oh, and tell them to coordinate with Grace Lamont of Price, Feinstein and Lamont. I owe her one, Lucius."

16

The next week passed relatively uneventfully in Gotham City. Dick worked with Alfred to improve his go game in the time remaining before he returned to college; Bruce fended off Roland Daggett's attacks stateside, while keeping an eye on developments overseas. He began to relax when no more break-ins were reported at Wayne subsidiaries.

Halfway around the world from Wayne Manor, the crescent moon gleamed like a delicate ivory carving above the city of Gotojin, a metropolis on the northwest shore of the island of Honshu that was often referred to as "the Empress of the Northern Coast." The city itself shone with its usual eclectic mix of traditional paper lanterns and blazing neon under the crystal-cold night sky. The volcanic cone of Mount Kajiiki, Gotojin's ancient and occasionally unstable consort, loomed on the city's western horizon, its crater glowing faintly against the frozen darkness.

Warm light flickered from the white paper shoji windows of Master Yoru's martial arts studio, located on the outskirts of the city within sight of the fitful volcano.

Inside the dojo, a lone student practiced the series of fighting dances known as katas.

Clad in a white *gi* jacket and cotton pants, the young woman whirled, punched, and kicked as she took on an array of imaginary opponents. Her occasional grunts of effort were the only sounds in the dojo. A ring of white candles had been arranged around the room; the lithe figure extinguished one of the tiny flames with each kick or swipe of her hand. At length all the candles but one had been snuffed out. As Kairi Nakano swung around to fend off the attack of the final phantom warrior, her eyes passed over the outside doorway. She gave a small gasp and froze in shock.

Standing in the entranceway was a tall man dressed entirely in black, his face obscured by a hooded mask. A sword hung from the red sash at his waist.

The Ninja stood for a moment in the flickering candle light. Then he prowled into the dojo like a great cat sidling toward its prey, his stiffened hands dancing in the hypnotic patterns which the night assassins called *kuji-kiri*.

"Who are you?" Kairi shook her head to clear it. "What do you want?"

"The pleasure of your company, woman." From his size she had thought he might be a *gaijin*, a foreigner—but his Japanese was as free of accent as her own. "Come, little flower—let us dance."

He gave an ironic bow, and the two fell into battle stances, circling the empty space between them as unconsciously as twin planets orbiting an invisible sun. They glided carefully through a dozen poses of attack and defense as they circled, each warily taking the measure of the other.

"*Hai!*" The Ninja's mask and hood helped to conceal his intentions, and his attack took Kairi by surprise. Darting at her across the floor, the large man launched a powerful kick and a back fist at the same time. Kairi dodged the kick, blocked the punch, and attempted a counterblow in quick succession. She was in turn blocked by the Ninja. A total of six seconds had passed by the time the combatants sprang apart and faced each other.

"Surprisingly good!" The Ninja gave a brittle laugh. "But sadly for you, little flower, not good enough."

Stung, Kairi worked to keep her mind free of anger. She assumed a crane stance, her eyes on the dark eyes of her opponent, visible in the narrow cutout across the upper portion of his face. Again he lunged, and again she read the move a split second too late. A single slashing kick and Kairi lay doubled up on the floor, the Ninja looming above her.

The tall man bent and checked the pulse point at her throat. With a nod, he hoisted the inert woman over one shoulder. Then he plucked a small parchment scroll tied with a black ribbon from his jacket and tossed it almost negligently onto a nearby tatami. He carried the woman out of the building and into the cold autumn night.

Two hours later, in a smaller dojo on the other side of Gotojin, Kairi sat tied to a wooden chair

with an intricate overlay of knotted rope. The
Ninja stood nearby with his back to her. The gym
was appointed much like Master Yoru's, though
on a smaller scale. Racked swords, punching dum-
mies, and anatomical charts filled the dingy space.

"Why have you done this?" Kairi asked the tall
man for the third time. He had been staring out
the window since their arrival, apparently lost in
thought. Now he turned to her as if once more
aware of her presence. He reached up and pulled
back his hood, revealing a darkly smiling face.

"For three reasons," Kyodai Ken told her.
"To settle an old debt. To make the next move in
the game." He was ticking them off on his black-
gloved fingers. "And to become the greatest
fighter the world has ever known."

Kairi shook her head, not understanding.
"You are an insane man," she said softly.

Kyodai gave a growling laugh. "No," he told
her. "I am merely a man who likes to win."

Master Yoru entered his studio with the morning
sun, a heavy cloak clasped for warmth about his
thin shoulders. A furrow appeared in his brow as
he surveyed the starkly furnished room: something was out of place. Then he noticed the tiny
scroll lying on the mat and moved to pick it up.
He unrolled it with trembling fingers, his face
tightening with dismay as he read the brief message.

17

Nighttime in the Batcave beneath Wayne Manor.

Batman and Robin were preparing to go out on patrol. Carrying his cowl under his arm, Bruce strode toward the Batmobile to join Robin, who was adjusting his mask in the black, mirrorlike surface of the vehicle. "I want to check out the Townsend District tonight," he told the younger man. "There's been an odd pattern of break-ins there that bears looking into." He lifted the black cowl in his hands and began to pull it down over his head.

The elevator door opened and Alfred stepped out into the cavern. "Master Bruce!" he called, "you have a telephone call. Long distance."

Bruce turned, surprise showing on his face as he peeled the mask off. What call would be important enough for Alfred to interrupt his departure? Something in the butler's face made him turn and walk to meet the older man.

"It's from Master Yoru," Alfred said quietly. His face was pale. "It doesn't seem to be good news."

Bruce's eyes narrowed. "I've been half expecting this." He walked to an extension and picked up the receiver. *"Konnichi-wa, Yoru Sensei . . ."*

Bruce spoke into the phone in quiet tones, listened for a few minutes, then spoke again. His face was somber when he hung up the phone and turned to Alfred.

"You'd better get the luggage out," he said. "We're going to Japan."

"All *right*!" Robin clapped his gloved hands together. Bruce whirled around to see the young man standing a few feet behind him. "When do we leave?"

"I was speaking about Alfred and myself," Bruce told him sternly. "This is a business trip, not a pleasure jaunt. You'd only—"

"Have the opportunity," Robin interjected smoothly, "to attend the largest annual go tournament held anywhere in the world—not to mention being able to soak up the local culture while you guys take care of business, *and* get the jump on the accelerated introductory Japanese class I signed up for at State this fall." He raised his palms as Bruce started to respond. "Look—you let me tag along and I promise I'll stay out of your hair. You know business bores me. You won't even realize I'm there."

"If I may venture to say so, sir," Alfred put in, "it would seem to be an ideal opportunity for Master Dick to get a head start on some of his studies." He cleared his throat as Bruce shot him a sharp look. *"If* I may venture to say so, that is . . ."

Bruce weighed the options silently for a long

moment. Then he gave a short nod. "All right, then. On the condition that you stick strictly to the itinerary Alfred and I work out for you."

Robin gave him a thumbs-up. "You got it, partner." He turned and bowed theatrically in the direction of the tunnel to the outside world. "*Sayonara,* Gotham City—*bonjour,* Japan!"

Bruce sighed. "Luggage for three," he told Alfred.

18

The private jet arced like a gleaming dart above the vast expanse of the Pacific. The interior of the plane resembled a small living room, with a kitchenette on one side. Dick was dozing with a book on his lap on one of the main cabin's roomy couches, while Alfred made tea in the kitchenette. Bruce sat in a plush seat and looked out through the window at the glittering, wind-rumpled water below. He doodled on a pad with a pencil.

Alfred set a tray of tea and rice cakes on a foldout table next to Bruce. "I should enjoy our return to Nippon considerably more, were it not for this unfortunate business," he said softly.

"So would I, Alfred." Bruce glanced at Dick, who seemed deep in slumber. "Especially since I agreed to let Dick accompany us. I hope you've come up with enough distractions to keep him busy and out of danger." He settled back in his seat. "At any rate, *giri* cannot be denied in this situation."

"*Giri* . . ." Alfred pursed his lips. "Ah, yes. Honor. Duty. Obligation." He gave Bruce a look of fond approval. "I cannot think of a single situation in which you have ever denied *giri*, Master Bruce."

The intercom crackled. "We'll be landing at the Gotojin Airport within the hour, Mr. Wayne," said the pilot.

Bruce returned his gaze to the pad on his lap as Alfred began to pour tea into small bowls of blue-and-white porcelain. He had sketched an elaborate image on the paper: a sinuous dragon coiled in demonic fury.

19

I t was early evening when they touched down in Gotojin.

Bruce's contact in the city was a plump young woman named Yasuko Moto, a representative of the largest of Wayne Enterprises' Japanese subsidiaries. She met them at the gate with a small entourage and an armful of white lilies.

The airport itself was furnished in basic international style, not all that different from what they had left behind in Gotham. Dick began to get the feeling that he was truly in another country when the introductions were conducted in rapid Japanese and accompanied by several bows on the part of each individual. Noticing the bewildered look on his face, Yasuko laid her hand on his arm and said in careful English: "Richard-*san*, your friends inform me that you have recently developed a strong interest in the playing of go. I am pleased to introduce to you my sister, Mariko, who shares your fascination. If you are planning to attend the tournament in Kyoto, Mariko will be honored to serve as your guide."

Dick grinned broadly. "Fantastic!" He stuck his hand out to the striking woman in her early twenties who stood holding a clipboard at Yasuko's side. "Pleased to meet you, Mariko."

"Excuse me. That is my secretary, Miss Yamanaka." Yasuko leaned past the attractive assistant and motioned to a thin girl of about fourteen, who had been watching the proceedings with a look of patient boredom. "This is Mari. She will gladly be your guide."

"Oh, great—thanks." Dick nodded unenthusiastically at Mariko. "But, hey, if it's too much trouble—"

"Not trouble." The girl lowered her eyes with a shy smile. "But please excusing my *Igirisu*—my English. He not very well."

"That's okay." He summoned a smile. "My Japanese is nonexistent. Hey—" He craned his neck past the young girl's shoulder to stare in the direction of one of the other gates. A herd of passengers had emerged from a recently landed commercial flight. "That looks like—" His look of surprise faded as friends and relatives mobbed the new arrivals, and the crowd streamed quickly through the terminal on their way to the baggage claim. He shook his head. "Nah, couldn't be," he said. Mariko had a questioning look on her thin face when he turned back to her. "Thought I saw somebody I recognized," Dick told her. "But I think it was just a trick of the light."

The visitors were delivered by limousine to the Gotojin Grand Imperator. The hotel was a combination of traditional Japanese architecture and Western high rise: a serene skyscraper with a high, peaked roof. The go tournament was scheduled to begin in Kyoto in two days. Yasuko assured Dick that her sister would be waiting for him at the gates of the civic center pavilion in Kyoto.

After a superb dinner in the hotel restaurant—which specialized, to Dick's surprise, in first-rate French cuisine—Alfred and Dick retired to their suite. Bruce had arranged to meet with Master Yoru early the next morning. In the meantime, he took a cab into the city to pay a brief courtesy call on the CEO of his main Japanese subsidiary.

"At eight-thirty in the evening?" Dick asked, amazed. "Haven't they ever heard of nine to five here?"

"We are in a different culture," Alfred reminded the young man as he showed him where to find the carefully concealed furniture in his seemingly empty room. They had taken a large suite which was divided into three bedrooms and a common sitting room, each separated from the others by a door of opaque paper.

Alfred had planned a series of sight-seeing trips for himself and Dick. "We can begin by exploring Kyoto tomorrow while Master Bruce conducts business," he told the young man. "That way you will be at least somewhat familiar with the city by the commencement of the tournament." Once the go tournament started, Dick was to remain in Kyoto on his own for three days.

Bruce returned to the hotel after his meeting with Mr. Tanaka of Wayne Industries Nippon. It was late, and Alfred and Dick were already in their respective rooms. Bruce sat for a minute on the firm futon Alfred had arranged for him. Then he silently donned his black-and-gray costume and stepped to the window.

The suite was located on the twelfth floor. Batman slid the window open and looked out over the panorama of lights and movement that was Gotojin at midnight. Another hotel towered about fifty feet away from the Gotojin Grand Imperator. Two stories beneath Bruce's window, a sturdy-looking flagpole jutted out from a decorative cornice on the other building. Batman inspected it with a tight smile of anticipation, his eyes traveling to a shorter building situated near the two hotels, and from there to a stand of regal-looking trees. He pulled himself quietly up onto the windowsill and drew out his grapple gun.

Five minutes later a dark shadow flitted unseen above the streets and alleyways of the city of Gotojin. There were those who went on sightseeing tours to acclimate themselves to unfamiliar surroundings, Batman reflected, as he swung and leaped above the gleaming city. Others chose a more challenging route.

20

atman made his way through the steel and
neon canyons of the unfamiliar city, retrac-
ing the route his taxi had taken him to the
Japanese headquarters of Wayne Enterprises. As he swung and climbed above the
streets, he began to notice a long black car that
was traveling more or less the same route. He followed it curiously and was not surprised to see it
pull around to the service entrance of the large
building.

Four men got out. One lounged against the
front fender of the car, a small radio transmitter in
his hand. The other three were dressed in ninja
fashion, all in black, with identical red sashes at
their waists and black masks over their faces. Batman watched from his hiding place as they used
ropes to scale the outside of the towering structure. It didn't take the Dark Knight long to deter-
mine that none of these men was Kyodai Ken.
Their movements were more awkward, less polished. He watched with interest as they jimmied
open a dark window on the fifth floor of the
building and silently slipped inside, one by one.

Batman remembered the tour he had been given of the building earlier that evening. Mr. Tanaka had told him that floors one through ten were all laid out identically. He searched his memory for the configuration of the corridor into which the three false ninja had entered, then circled around to the other side of the building, away from the eyes and ears of the man who waited by the black limo. Firing his grapple gun, he rose swiftly to the fifth floor. It was a simple matter to gain access through one of the windows. Soon he found himself in a long corridor lit only by the red glow of an exit sign at the far end. He padded softly down the hallway to where it branched off to the right and left. He listened for a moment, then chose the right-hand route.

He tracked the faint sounds to the partially open door of an office midway down the corridor. Pale light shone from a small lantern that had been set in the middle of the carpeted floor. Peering in, he saw one of the black-clad men leaning against a receptionist's desk. He had pulled up the bottom of his mask and was speaking softly into a small radio transceiver—no doubt to the fourth man who waited down at the car. Batman flattened himself against the corridor wall and listened.

"Nah," the man was saying. "It went off without a hitch. Ray and Miguel are crackin' the safe right now. Once we get the bonds, we'll scatter a buncha them little throwing stars around the place and get outta here." A string of small crackling sounds came from the radio. The hoodlum listened, nodding his head.

"Yeah, boss, sure. Okay—over and out." The hoodlum ran the antenna back into the radio and pulled his mask down over his chin. He slid off the edge of his desk and turned toward the other room. Someone tapped him on the shoulder.

When the men identified as Ray and Miguel emerged from the inner office, they were greeted by the sight of their confederate trussed up with thin line and lying facedown across the receptionist's desk.

"Hey!" Ray said, pulling out his revolver. "Dano, izzat you—?" There was a whirring sound and a small black object shaped like a scalloped batwing crossed the room and whirled around the two crooks. It was trailing a thin cord. After half a dozen turns the line was pulled taut, yanking the two into one another. Their foreheads smacked together with the hollow sound of two coconuts colliding.

The man waiting by the limo stubbed out his cigarette and adjusted his collar against the cool night air. He was a tall, sharply dressed man with a long face and tired eyes. He checked his wristwatch and thumbed the switch on his radio. "Dano?" he said. "How're you guys doin'?"

"Not too well," said a husky voice from the other side of the limo. "Unless you consider being knocked unconscious and tied up a mark of success."

"What?" The tall man whirled around, hand groping inside his trench coat.

A black-cloaked figure vaulted over the limo's roof, snatched the gun from the crook's fingers and whirled him around to flatten him face first against the side of the car.

"*Not* a good idea," came the chilling voice. "Guns can go off at the most unexpected moments." Gloved hands patted him down efficiently, removing a smaller revolver and a wicked-looking knife. "*Tsk*. Somebody's bound to get hurt with an arsenal like this." The dark figure spun him around into the streetlight. "Well, well. Mr. Crocker. Fresh out of prison and already so far from home."

"Jeez!" Crocker's mouth gaped open. "What're *you* doin' here?"

"I might ask you the same question—but I think I already know the answer." The Dark Knight opened the front door of the limo and shoved Crocker inside. Then he produced a length of thin line and began to wrap it around the hoodlum's hands. "Seems there's no lengths your boss won't go to in order to cause trouble for people he doesn't like." He fastened the bound wrists securely to the steering wheel, then reached around beneath them and removed the car keys. "Tell Mr. Daggett the next time you talk to him that I'll be watching his moves twice as closely from now on—no matter what country he decides to do his moving in."

Batman slammed the door shut, then leaned into the half-open window. "Oh, and Crocker—if I were you, I'd hope the cops found me and my cut-rate ninjas before the local gangsters did. I hear the *yakuza* are rather touchy about outsiders muscling in on their territory. . . ."

The Dark Knight stepped away from the car

and searched the shadows at the base of the nearby buildings. He had the impression that someone was watching him, but it was only a fleeting sensation. He fired his grappling gun and took off into the night.

21

Bruce arrived at Master Yoru's dojo with the dawn. The martial arts school commanded an excellent view of both the sprawling city on one side and the volcanic dome of Mount Kajiiki on the other.

Bruce had climbed the gently winding path to the school with a mixture of nostalgia and foreboding. He and Master Yoru had exchanged warm greetings. Now Bruce stood with the *sensei* next to an open window on the south side of the dojo and looked out at the expanse of city and mountain. The distant lights of Gotojin were only just beginning to flicker and die as darkness faded from the city.

"They say there has been renewed volcanic activity," Yoru said, turning to gaze bleakly at the softly glowing crater. "People are being warned to stay off the slopes." He sighed. "It is a time of great upheaval in many matters."

A young Japanese man with a black belt around his *gi* led a class of four students in sparring and tumbling practice on the mats in the center of the room. Master Yoru allowed his attention to focus on the students while Bruce studied the scroll left by Kyodai Ken. "Again, Satomi!" the old man called to a stocky young woman who had just tossed her sparring partner onto the mat. "It should not seem so forced. Let the movements flow through you." He nodded his approval as the hapless victim was hurled to the mat again seconds later. "Better . . ."

Bruce looked up from the scroll. "He wrote that he would contact you on the fourth day from the kidnapping. That would be the day after to-morrow. Why the delay, I wonder?" He released a deep breath. "Of course I will help in any way that I can, *Sensei*." His Japanese was precise and formal. His eyes rested with curiosity on the old man's face. "But I must ask—what made you think of calling me?"

"You cannot hide the warrior spirit behind your playboy image, Bruce-*san*," Yoru said. "Ky-odai Ken returned from America in defeat."

Bruce pretended to examine a small spot of dust on the sleeve of his jacket. "Yet it was the Batman who defeated him," he commented.

"So it is said." The old man wore an enig-matic smile. "Perhaps I thought you might some-how be able to enlist the aid of this . . . Batman." He turned back to the window. "You are acquainted with him, are you not?"

Bruce pursed his lips. "We've met. . . ."

"Then please allow me to tell you a brief story, Bruce-*san*." The old man lowered himself onto one of the tatami mats at the edge of the room, motioning his guest to do likewise. "If you deem it worthy of his attention, perhaps you will see fit to pass the tale along to your acquaintance. . . ."

Outside, what was left of the city's myriad colored lights seemed outmatched by the faint orange glow flickering above the rim of the crater, as though a great dragon lay coiled in uneasy slumber not far from the unsuspecting cityfolk.

22

When Alfred and Dick awoke after their first
night in Japan, they discovered that Bruce
was already up and out of the suite. Alfred
had decided that the pair would take the
bullet train from Gotojin to Kyoto. Dick
squinted through the train's large window for the
first half of the trip, trying to get a sense of the
countryside as it rushed past him at a blurred 270
kilometers an hour. Finally he gave up, turning his
attention instead to the small English/Japanese
phrase book Alfred had obtained for him.

They left the station in Kyoto and went directly to their lodgings for the night: a traditional
guesthouse that Alfred judged had been constructed during the late 1800s. As in the Grand
Imperator, the rooms seemed stark to Dick,
floored with tatami and bare of furniture, with
futons concealed in the closet.

Sliding doors opened onto a panorama of
beautifully tended gardens. "The Flowering
City," Alfred announced with a grand sweep of
his folded umbrella. After the pair had freshened
up, the innkeeper brought them a snack of ele-

gantly prepared sashimi. Donning garden slippers provided by their hosts, they rested in the court-yard for an hour before embarking on an explora-tion of the city and its surroundings.

Alfred conducted Dick on a tour of memora-ble sights in surprising combinations. At one point they crossed an ancient bridge arching over a meandering stream, only to stop at a pickle shop on the other side, where Alfred obtained free sam-ples of a variety of brine-soaked delicacies.

Chattering schoolchildren in bright uniforms swept past them like flocks of birds as they climbed Storm Mountain on a winding trail. While Alfred rested briefly on a bench partway up the slope, Dick took a handful of Japanese coins from his pocket and went to a vending machine he had spied at the side of the path. He returned empty-handed. "I was hoping for peanut butter crackers or maybe a package of M & Ms," he re-ported to Alfred, "but the machine was full of beer and sake!"

The older man nodded sagely. "We are indeed in another country, Master Dick."

Returning to the heart of the city, they stopped for an early dinner in an upscale restau-rant. Alfred ordered for both of them, as Dick surveyed the airy room with its paper lanterns and low tables. As their first course was arriving, they heard a shocked exclamation from the neighbor-ing table. A portly couple whose clothing and identical blond pageboy haircuts identified them as tourists, had summoned their waitress, pointing frantically at the dish set between them.

Dick was sitting too far away to make out

BATMAN: THE DRAGON AND THE BAT 101

much of the conversation—which sounded to his straining ears as if it were not being conducted in English. Alfred craned his neck discreetly, then reported back to Dick. "It appears that they ordered the haji fish, a delicacy which is served in a simple yet very elegant fashion at this restaurant: partially dismembered on a bed of lettuce."

"Sounds delightful," Dick commented. "So what's the problem? Not enough ketchup?"

Alfred pursed his lips. "Apparently the fish was so fresh as to still be engaged in its death throes when it arrived at their table. From what the red-faced gentleman was saying, I gather that this is not how they are used to having their seafood served back home in Düsseldorf."

"Death throes?" Dick pushed back from the table and examined his own plate for the first time. "Uh, Alfred, you want to check this out? I think I just saw part of my own entree starting to twitch."

"Highly unlikely, Master Dick," the butler reassured him, "unless tofu and water chestnuts have evolved considerably since my last trip to Kyoto."

Dick was forced to accept Alfred's word on the deceased state of the rest of their meal: raw shellfish, soybean soup, and a rainbow of artfully carved vegetables that he at first mistook for a flower arrangement.

On their way back to the guesthouse, the pair stopped at a large flea market which, Alfred claimed, was held only on the twenty-fifth day of each month. There they spent a leisurely hour prowling among offerings of antique phono-

graphs, fresh sugar cane, hand-painted scrolls dating from the Edo period, and used silk kimonos.
At one stall Dick hefted a small bowl with a delicate blue-green glaze. "Hey, I kind of like this,"
he told his companion. "I was thinking of getting
a little souvenir to send to Ellie back at Haly's Big
Top." He balanced it on his fingertips as he inspected the finish. "Can you ask how much it is?"

Alfred conversed briefly with the stout man
behind the counter. "Mr. Sato applauds your exquisite taste, Master Dick, and is willing to let you
have that particular example of Aokutani pottery
for a mere eight hundred and fifty dollars."

"Yikes!" Dick clasped the bowl in both hands
and returned it gingerly to the counter. "Maybe
she'd like a nice scarf . . ."

A little boy of six or seven was perched on a
stool near the flea market's exit, dangling his bare
toes a few inches above a half-filled tub of water.
In the tub, four small turtles sat on an island made
from an overturned flower pot. "You like my
fighting turtle?" the boy asked Dick as they
paused by the tub.

"Fighting turtles?" Dick squatted down and
peered into the tub. Four pairs of green-lidded
eyes looked placidly up at him. "What makes you
think they're fighting turtles?"

The little boy drew himself up. "I train them
myself, every day. Work very hard."

"Miniature masters of the martial arts, huh?"
Dick grinned down at the reptiles. A small dab of
color in the center of each shell distinguished the
turtles from one another. "What are their
names?"

"Larry, Curly, Moe." The boy indicated them with a short length of bamboo. "That little one called Shemp."

Dick blinked. "Those don't sound much like ninja names to me."

"They're not *ninja,*" the boy said indignantly. He hopped off the stool. "Look." Grasping Dick's hand, he brought it down to within an inch of the turtles' heads. The quartet regarded the intrusion with mild interest, but made no move to defend their territory.

"Look at what?" Dick withdrew his hand. "They just sat there."

"Just so. They are samurai turtles. Very honorable. Never fight unless good reason."

"So how much are you asking for these honorable fighting turtles?" Dick asked as he got to his feet. "It must be hard to give up such well-trained warriors."

"Not give." The little boy resumed his perch on the stool. "Rent. Five hundred yen for one day. You take them home, let them swim in fish pond, bring back to my house tomorrow."

"Rental turtles. Interesting idea." Dick glanced at Alfred. "I don't suppose our guesthouse would let us keep them in the bathtub overnight, would it?"

"I shouldn't think so," the butler replied, "even if it weren't a communal bath."

"Communal?" Dick's jaw dropped. "You didn't say anything about communal when we checked in."

"Bathtub no good anyway," the boy declared. "Only fish pond. Here." The young merchant

motioned Dick closer. "I tell you my idea. Some-
body rents my turtles, takes home to fish pond.
Turtles eat one, two fish, have a very good time.
Next day bring them back, I rent again. This way
I make money, never have to buy turtle food."

"I get it!" Dick straightened with a laugh.
"Alfred, I think we're looking at a future chief
executive officer here." He drew a handful of
coins from his pocket. "Here—seed money. Look
me up when you've made your first million yen."

"*Arigato.*" The boy bowed gravely. "Very
good idea." He cocked a hopeful eye at Alfred.
"You like to give me seed, too? I know a lake full
of turtles, too many for one boy. Soon need more
partners . . ."

23

A steady rain fell outside the Gotojin Grand Imperator, slowing traffic and softening the city sounds that rose around the towering building.

Bruce sat cross-legged in front of the futon in his sparsely appointed room. Smoke drifted from an incense burner glowing in the corner. Bruce's eyes were closed. He took deep, regular breaths.

There was a light tapping of knuckles on wood. Bruce opened his eyes. "Come."

The fragile-looking connecting door slid open, and Alfred entered the room. He was dressed in a colorful kimono patterned with red and white cranes, the black garters that held up his socks clearly visible above his slippers. He carried a porcelain teapot and two shallow cups on a bamboo tray.

"Welcome back." Bruce wiped the back of his hand across his eyes. "Did you get Dick settled in Kyoto?" he asked.

"Indeed. We found a lovely little inn dating back to the Meiji era. Excellent sashimi. Master

Dick was a bit uneasy about the bathing arrangements, but I reminded him that he had stated quite emphatically his wish to 'soak up the local culture' upon our arrival." Alfred nodded his head toward the bamboo tray in his hands. "A spot of tea before retiring, Master Bruce? The farmer's market down the road has an excellent selection, and I have managed to come into possession of a marvelous green brew."

"No thanks, Alfred." Bruce spread his arms wide and leaned back against the futon. "I'm about to turn in."

"Of course." Alfred nodded and turned to leave. He paused in the doorway. "Master Bruce, if I may be so bold—how did your meeting with Master Yoru go?"

"It wasn't good news." Bruce dropped his arms to his sides and pushed himself up from the floor. He stretched with a groan. "I believe I will have that tea, after all, Alfred. Are you in the mood for a bedtime story before you retire?"

The butler raised his brows quizzically as he poured the other man a small cup of steaming yellow-green liquid. Bruce held the saucer in his palm and looked down into the cup as if peering through the tea leaves into another age.

Alfred set the tray on a low table and settled on the edge of the futon as Bruce started to pace the room.

"Five hundred years ago," he began, "there dwelt in this region a certain fighting man of great attainment. He was a philosopher as well as a warrior, a scholar of high accomplishment, and he alone had taught himself how to manipulate the *ki* lines—the currents of life force that course through a person's body. Rather than using needles, as the Chinese do with acupuncture, this man employed precise blows of his knuckles and fingertips against the body's pressure points. He called the art *kiba-no-hoko*, 'the Way of the Fang.' " Bruce shifted his stance and lifted his hands unconsciously as he spoke, reaching out with light taps of his fingers to repel a horde of imaginary attackers as he paced the room. Alfred watched through half-closed eyes, almost able to see the unfortunate foes as they were sent flying, one after the other, to crash against the floor and walls.

"But the *kiba-no-hoko* was so efficient and so terrible that this Master soon decided it was too dangerous to teach," Bruce continued. "The gentle taps of the Fang could render a man unconscious or permanently disabled. There was even a certain touch that was instantly fatal.

"Now the Master had inscribed the secrets of the Way of the Fang on a single scroll. He took the only copy of this record and hid it in one of the thousand caves that honeycomb the slopes of Mount Kajiiki." Bruce was staring at the bare wall, his head tilted slightly to one side as if the scene he was describing were painted there. "During his lifetime he revealed the location to no one but his eldest son. When the old man died, his son passed the secret of the scroll's location to his own son. And so it has gone for five hundred years."

Alfred leaned forward on the edge of the futon, feeling like a schoolboy again, enthralled by tales of Stevenson and Kipling. "And Master Yoru . . . ?"

"Yoru *Sensei* is the great-great-great grandson of the man who created the forbidden art. He is also the only man alive who knows the location of the hidden scroll." Bruce sipped his tea reflectively. "Yoru *Sensei* has no sons. When he leaves this world, the secret of the *kiba-no-hoko* goes with him." He moved toward the window and looked out. The rain continued unabated. Neon reflections glimmered from puddles in the cobblestone street below. Across the street was a combination pachinko and video game parlor, the old once again blending with the new. A blue neon dragon gleamed above the door of the establishment, a puff of fluorescent orange flame blinking on and off above its nostrils.

Alfred got to his feet and came to the window behind Bruce. "A fascinating tale," he said quietly. "And the kidnapped young lady?"

"Yoru's star pupil," Bruce told the older man. "Her name is Kairi Nakano. Kyodai Ken proposes to trade her for knowledge of the location of the scroll. He needs the scroll so that he can employ the Way of the Fang against Batman."

"*Batman* . . ." Alfred wore a puzzled frown. "Why should he wish to harm Batman? You defeated the Ninja as Bruce Wayne."

"Kyodai has fought me both as Bruce Wayne and as Batman," Bruce said grimly. "To an expert, fighting styles are like fingerprints. I am sure this is why he told Master Yoru he would not be contacting him again until tomorrow. He wanted to give Yoru time to contact me and convince me to come over here. The Ninja knows that we are the same man."

24

Dick had almost forgotten about Yasuko Moto's shy little sister by the time he arrived at the gates of the civic pavilion that was hosting the go tournament. He had gotten up early in hopes of having the communal bath to himself; at 5 A.M. the only other inhabitants had been an elderly man and woman who, thankfully, had kept to their own end of the steaming pool.

After a light breakfast—during which he earned the disapproval of his server by dousing his rice with so much soy sauce that it resembled a ball of muddy swamp roots—Dick left the guesthouse for the civic center. He managed to get lost twice, despite the map Alfred had drawn for him, and ended up obtaining directions from an elderly woman by repeating the word "go" over and over until she pointed him down the correct street.

The pavilion was a low, circular building surrounded by careful landscaping. Dick felt a light tap on his arm as he hurried up to the entrance. Turning, he stared at the thin young girl in jeans and T-shirt for several seconds before making the connection with their meeting at the airport.

"Mariko-*san*!" He attempted a bow. "Nice to see you." He nodded toward the ticket window as he reached for his wallet. "Have you gotten your ticket yet? Let me—"

"Ticket? Already two." She showed him a pair of magenta rectangles covered with Japanese writing. "One you. One me."

"Oh, hey, I can't let you do that." He pulled out his billfold and flipped it open. "How much were they?"

She set her hand on his. "From company. Your friend Wayne-*san* big important man. My sister proud give you ticket for go tournament."

"Well, okay." He returned the wallet reluctantly to his back pocket. "But I'm buying the popcorn."

The pavilion was large, but the area in which the main action of the tournament was to take place was relatively small. Four low tables had been erected, each one occupied by a go board and bracketed by a pair of simple kneeling mats. A wide circle of bleachers surrounded the playing area. Mariko located their seats, which were on the bottom row, only a few yards from one of the tables, while Dick made his way through the gathering spectators to the nearest concession stand. He returned to his seat holding a small paper container at arm's length. "The closest they came to popcorn was eel and fish eggs," he told Mariko. "I won't be upset if you don't want any."

"No, no. Tasty!" The girl eagerly accepted the

tiny box and the pair of disposable chopsticks that came with it. "You half?" she asked.

"No—please. Feel free to enjoy the whole thing." Dick turned his attention to the center of the pavilion as his companion attacked her snack with evident relish. A group of perhaps fifteen individuals was conferring in low tones at the edge of the playing area. All but two of them were men, ranging in age from early thirties to a bald, bent-backed gentleman who could have been anywhere from seventy to over a hundred. One of the women was middle-aged, and the other was a few years older than Dick. "I wonder if any of them is the reigning champ," he murmured to himself, leaning his elbows on his knees.

"Actually," piped a youthful voice at his side, "only about half that bunch are competitors. The rest are teachers and novices. They're here to give moral support—or pick up pointers. Cheerleaders and groupies, you might call them."

"Oh yeah? And how do you . . ." Dick's words trailed off as he turned to the source of the utterance. To his amazement the bench to his left was empty except for Mariko, who was probing industriously with her chopsticks in the bottom of the container. She popped the last glistening morsel of eel into her mouth and looked up at him with a sunny smile. "Of course," she continued, "in the old days there was a lot more riding on the game. Did you know that back in the late 1800s in San Francisco, Japanese immigrants used to wager money on go games, and that sometimes disputes over who won would escalate into violence? You've seen that little cutout section on the bottom of the more expensive boards that's supposed to make the stones resonate better when you click them down? *I* heard that was originally used to catch the blood when one of the players would get fed up with a kibitzer and cut his head off with their sword." She set the container down and wiped her mouth on the back of a thin wrist. "Didn't know that, huh?"

"Wait a minute here . . ." Dick used his fingertip to push his gaping jaw shut. "All of a sudden you sound more American than I do! What happened to 'excusing my English, he not very well'?"

"We'd only just met," Mariko said reasonably. "I hadn't made up my mind about you yet. You wouldn't believe the losers I've gotten stuck with, the other times Suki's asked me to play friendly little guide to her foreign visitors. I've found it helps keep the interactions to a minimum if they think there's a language barrier."

Dick was flabbergasted. "So now I'm being evaluated by fourteen-year-old girls to see if I'm worth talking to!"

"Fifteen last month," Mariko said. "What kind of music do you like?"

"Huh? Different things. Mostly rock. A little jazz. Classical." He shrugged. "I've been in a real Mozart phase lately. Why?"

Mariko stretched her legs out in front of her and leaned back on the bench. "I like Vaughan Williams when I'm feeling classical. I thought Joni Mitchell's latest album showed a long-overdue return to her roots. My favorite heavy metal group is Metallica, and my most recent soundtrack purchase was an old LP of Bernard Herrmann. Did you ever hear his film score to *Jason and the Argonauts*? So evocative! I can see those stop-motion skeletons perfectly every time I play it. Harryhausen may be a bit passé in this day of computer animation, but I still get a thrill from his work." She smiled appreciatively and sat up straight. "What kind of movies do you like?"

"How do you *do* that?" Dick shook his head in amazement. "How do you manage to talk so much without stopping to breathe?"

"It's all in the nose," Mariko said sagely. "Speak with the mouth, breathe with the nose. If you want some more eel you'd better get it now, because the first match is about to begin." She patted the bench between them. "I'll save your place."

Dick returned to the concession stand and purchased two more eel-and-egg containers. When he came back to the bench Mariko was engaged in animated conversation with the ancient-looking man Dick had noticed standing with the others near the playing area.

She switched smoothly to English as Dick set the double order of eel down by her side: "—and besides, *Sensei,* I have to stay with this esteemed friend of my sister. He's a very important American visitor, as you can see from his haircut and shoes. His name is Richard."

"Dick." He stared down at his scuffed loafers. "What about my shoes?"

"Very nice," the old man told him in a quaking whisper. "Very hip." He made a final statement in Japanese to Mariko, emphasized his point by tapping a bony finger twice on her knee, and shuffled back to the group by the tables.

"He seemed pleasant," Dick said. "Friend of yours?"

Mariko shrugged her narrow shoulders. "More like a coach. I studied with him for a while when I was younger. Now every time I show up at a match, he asks me why I'm not competing."

"You play go? Professionally?"

"If I did, then Hideo *sensei* wouldn't have to ask me, would he?"

"Mariko Moto," Dick began, "you are without a doubt one of the most—"

"Hssst." She silenced him with a finger to his lips. "They're starting. They can get very cross if there's too much noise from the audience. Remember San Francisco." She leaned forward, settling her chin on her palms, as the first players took their places. "And call me Mari."

The matches were conducted simultaneously, with the seating arranged so that audience members could concentrate on the game that was taking place nearest to their bleachers. Dick began whispering questions to his seat mate after the first ten minutes of play. Soon Mari was supplying him with a running commentary—not just on the two players seated directly in front of them but on all four games at once. "See, those two on the right are both playing it cautious. That's why it seems like they're still in *fuseki,* when everyone else's gotten to the real fighting. . . . Oh, *that* was interesting—old Kawamura at the far table's trying a squeeze play, but it's very premature. . . . There, on the left, she's already got a *shicho* going.

If he can't break out of that zigzag, she's got him in permanent *atari*. . . ."

They took a break after the first two hours. Dick sat on a bench outside the pavilion with his forehead cradled in his palm, trying to organize the torrent of information he'd just absorbed. "Okay, Alfred's gonna want details. Tell me again. What's that *'me ari me nashi'* business again?"

"It's easy," Mari said. "Just think of it as a *semeai* in which one side's got an eye and the other doesn't."

"Oh, yeah," Dick muttered. "Easy as pie—as long as you're here to talk me through it. Now, are you sure you can make it tomorrow and the next day?"

"I told you, we're on holiday till next week." Her eye wandered to a folded newspaper sitting nearby on the bench. "Ah," she said. "Excitement in Gotojin."

Something about the front page photograph caught Dick's attention and he reached for the paper. "Hey." He ran his finger along a column of Japanese *hiragana* to the right of a picture of three black-clad men who had been bound with thin cord and lined up like sausages along the top of a desk. "What's this headline say?"

Mari took the paper from his hands and unfolded it.

"False ninja caught during corporate break-in," she translated. "Witnesses report sighting *koomori-no-kami* near crime scene."

Dick looked puzzled. "Koomori-no-kami?" he repeated.

"Spirit of the bat," said Mari.

25

Yoru had been instructed to expect a call from Kyodai Ken on the afternoon of Bruce's second full day in Japan.

Bruce rose early and worked out in the gym at the hotel. While Alfred frequented the scattering of small shops that surrounded the hotel, his employer took a taxi into the city's business district, where he conducted meetings with Tanaka and several of his associates. There Bruce received a disturbing report from Yasuko Moto: someone who had not wished to leave a name had made several calls over the last two days inquiring as to Bruce's scheduled whereabouts.

Bruce returned to the hotel after lunching at a sushi bar with the CEO of a powerful communications conglomerate. He arrived at the dojo an hour later, spending time observing the students at their work with Master Yoru while they waited for Kyodai to make contact. Bruce was admiring a recent variation on one of the throws Yoru had taught him years earlier, when the phone call finally came.

"Aa. Waka ta." Master Yoru set the receiver

on its cradle and turned to Bruce with a look of somber disgust. "It was Kyodai Ken. Even to speak with him leaves an unwholesome taste in my mouth."

"Did he give you instructions for the exchange?"

"*Hai*. It is to take place shortly after dark this evening, in the Uramachi District." Yoru made another sour face. "It is a bad part of town, a place of thieves and *yakuza*. A ninja would feel at home there."

Bruce hesitated. "You could supply him with a false map," he told his old mentor. "He wouldn't know the difference until after Kairi was safe."

"True." Yoru looked up at him. "But *I* would know. You are familiar with the code of *bushido*, Bruce-*san*. Ninja may lie and cheat as they will. Samurai must not." He handed his former pupil a rolled-up parchment tied with a red ribbon.

"*Hai, sensei.*" Bruce nodded. "*Wakarimasu*. I will see that the map is delivered." He bowed and left the dojo.

The Empress of the Northern Coast was resplendent in her finest neon jewelry that evening, colorful signs winking next to one another like a swarm of mechanical fireflies as they advertised the nightclubs, theaters, and massage parlors of the seedy section of Gotojin known as the Uramachi District.

The Ninja stood on a rooftop in the blinking red and green light of a tea shop sign. A mixture of smells rose to him through the dusk—some pleasant, others decidedly not. Kyodai held a short sword in one hand. In the other was the rope that led leashlike to Kairi Nakano, who stood a few feet away, her head bowed and her arms trussed securely behind her back.

"Yoru *Sensei* will not come," Kairi said softly.

"Most assuredly he will," Kyodai replied confidently. "You are more like his daughter than his student. *Giri* would compel him to come even if affection did not. He would do anything to save you."

"Let her go, ninja." The voice came like a sudden chill wind from behind them. The man in black released the rope that held Kairi and whirled around, eyes wide. Both his hands were locked on the hilt of his sword. *"You!"*

The Dark Knight stood outlined against the city lights at the edge of the roof, his cape fluttering in the night breeze.

"End this senseless game, Kyodai." The husky voice had a weary edge to it. He held up the beribboned map. "Let her go."

"Ah." Kyodai Ken's gaze fell on the scroll. He gave a short nod of understanding. "Old Yoru did as I hoped he would. I must remember to thank him for sending you to this rooftop. Now throw me the map!" His eyes were eager. He turned slightly, angling the tip of the sword in Kairi's direction with one hand as he stretched out the other in a beckoning gesture. "Throw it and she lives."

The Dark Knight remained motionless. "The young woman, first," he said.

The Ninja smiled behind his black face mask, his eyes riveted on the scroll. At his back, Kairi clenched her jaw in sudden determination. Taking advantage of her captor's distraction, she swung her right leg in a smooth arc and knocked the Ninja's feet out from under him. *"Hai!"* she cried triumphantly.

Kyodai Ken fell with a hoarse shout of surprise.

Batman lunged forward, moving with almost inhuman speed as he reached for the Ninja. Kyodai Ken rolled easily to his feet, throwing a vicious side kick at Kairi as she turned awkwardly to run, her arms still bound behind her back. The blow knocked her stumbling across the gritty surface of the rooftop. Her hips struck the low wall at the edge of the roof. Batman watched in horror as she fought for balance, teetered for a long moment, and tipped over the side.

The Dark Knight dived after her, losing his grip on the scroll as he cleared the low wall and sent himself hurtling downward.

Things were happening at a dizzying speed.

Batman fired his grapple gun with one hand, his other arm reaching out to encircle Kairi's waist. The grapple's trio of sharp hooks fastened around an ornamented protrusion on a nearby building and caught.

Kyodai Ken had also rushed to the edge of the rooftop. As his two enemies fell, he whipped a *kusari-kama* from his sash and sent the combination chain and throwing knife after the scroll. The knife's sharp point speared the roll of paper in midair. The Ninja reeled in the chain with a cry of triumph and ducked back from the edge of the roof.

Batman and Kairi swung like a double pendulum across the alley. The Dark Knight released the line at the last moment, dropping them heavily onto a balcony on the nearest building. He pushed to his feet and knelt over Kairi. "I am all right," she gasped as he used the sharp edge of a Batarang to slice through her bonds.

"Stay here!" he ordered. "I will return for you."

Kairi watched wide-eyed as the dark figure aimed his grapple at the rooftop and fired it again. There was a humming sound as the line hauled him upward. *"Koomori-no-kami,"* she murmured in awe, "Fly swiftly, Spirit of the Bat. . . ."

26

atman hauled himself onto the rooftop and looked around cautiously. The Ninja was nowhere to be seen. Then a flash of dark motion caught his eye and he spotted his adversary. The black figure stood at the edge of a roof two buildings away, staring back in the Dark Knight's direction as if waiting for Batman to notice him.

As the Dark Knight took off in pursuit, the Ninja leaped the gap between buildings and made his way along a third roof, his splayed limbs making him look like a spidery caricature of a human being as he ran silhouetted against the glow of city lights.

The distance between the two narrowed gradually as Batman leaped and swung after his prey, once more in his element among the shadowy rooftops. The Ninja glanced back over his shoulder, gauging his pursuer's progress. From a hidden pocket he pulled a handful of small, spiky objects that were shaped like children's jacks, but with razor-sharp points. He opened his hand as he hopped forward, scattering the vicious toys on the roof behind him with an evil chuckle.

Batman spotted the gleam of metal on the rooftop ahead of him. Racing forward, he leaped into the air and did a high front flip over the deadly objects. He landed beyond the sharp points and resumed his pursuit, smiling grimly to himself as he scanned the rooftops in front of him: the Ninja had apparently run out of buildings.

Kyodai Ken was well versed in the varied arts of the spy and assassin and had a few more options at his disposal. Pausing at the edge of the final rooftop, he drew on a pair of special gloves tipped with needle-sharp claws. Then he clambered over the side and began to crawl down the weathered wood like a giant spider. When the Dark Knight reached the edge of the building, the Ninja was no more than ten feet above the ground. Batman dived down into the darkness without hesitation, twisting to fire his grapple gun back up at the rooftop in mid-fall.

The Ninja dropped to the street and pulled half a dozen throwing stars from the folds of his black uniform. He hurled them upward at the figure looming above his head.

Swinging downward at the end of the line, Batman jerked his legs up as the *shuriken* whizzed toward him. The stars stabbed into the wall just beneath him.

Kyodai Ken sprang away from the wall and turned back. He held an odd-looking metal device in his black-gloved hand. At the touch of a button, a fine spray of oil began to coat the pavement at the base of the wall.

Batman pushed off from the bricks a few feet above the street and landed safely beyond the spreading patch of slickness. He sprinted after the black figure.

Kyodai Ken was breathing in gasps as Batman closed on him. The Dark Knight's pursuit had taken on the relentless quality of a nightmare. Kyodai spotted a dead-end alleyway up ahead and applied a last burst of speed to duck inside. He was waiting just past the alley's entrance, a short bamboo tube in his hand, when Batman swung around the corner. The Ninja gave the tube a sharp twist. There was a hiss, then an inky cloud of vapor spewed forth, an unfolding black miasma which began to spread rapidly throughout the alley.

The Dark Knight had darted back into the street at the sound of the hiss. He pulled a small breathing mask from his utility belt and clapped it over his nose and mouth, then moved cautiously forward into the vapor.

Thirty seconds later he pulled the filter from his face and scanned the thinning cloud in frustration. The alleyway was empty.

27

Batman returned to the balcony where he had left Kairi. Together they made their way to Master Yoru's dojo.

"The Ninja escaped with the map," the Dark Knight reported to the old man as they stood on the gentle slope outside the building. "I have no doubt that he will use it."

"Honor has been served," Yoru replied. His ancient eyes watched Batman closely. "And Kairi is safe. For this I am very grateful. You must feel free to return with my gratitude to America whenever you wish to do so."

"Not yet," Batman said. "First I must find the Ninja." He clasped hands with Yoru and departed the dojo.

"Who is this Spirit of the Bat?" the young woman asked her mentor, as she watched the Dark Knight melt into the shadows below the dojo.

Yoru gave a faint smile. "A friend," he told her.

"One does not often find a friend as remarkable as that one," Kairi whispered, shivering in the mild breeze. "But, *Sensei*—Kyodai Ken now has the directions to the secret cave."

"True," Yoru said, his eyes on the glowing crater that reared in the darkness to the west. "But so, too, does our remarkable friend."

28

A tiny spark of yellow light wavered up the dark flank of Mount Kajiiki. High above, at the lip of the crater, a faint red-orange glow pulsed against the night as the volcano slumbered fitfully.

Kyodai Ken held the lantern high as he neared the entrance to the cave. The night was chill, and he wore a blue quilted jacket incongruously over his black garments.

The murky darkness retreated before the shuddering yellow light. Kyodai moved into the cave and set the lantern down on the rock floor. Then he pulled the map from the folds of his costume.

Above him, the volcano grumbled once like an old man talking in his sleep, then fell silent. A moment later, it stirred again with more force, the little cavern quaking perceptibly as the Ninja squatted on his haunches to read the delicate characters on the map. He looked up, narrowing his eyes at the far wall, and pushed the scroll back into his pocket.

Lifting the lantern, Kyodai approached the

wall. Shadows stretched crazily away from him as he walked. Holding the light in his left hand, he pulled at a chunk of grayish rock midway up the wall with his right, pawing the packed dirt away from its sides and wiggling it loose. Finally the rock scraped free, revealing a shallow hole.

Kyodai set the lantern down again. The floor of the cave was still, yet his hands trembled as he eased an ornately carved wooden chest from its place of concealment. He fumbled the lid open with a gasp of triumph and snatched up the dusty scroll that lay inside. Lifting the tube of yellowed parchment into the lamplight, he began to unroll it.

The slow passage of centuries had left the paper thin and brittle. It came apart with a whisper of sound, crumbling into dusty fragments in the Ninja's hands. Kyodai Ken watched in horror as the pieces fluttered back into the box in a small snowstorm of rotted parchment.

The Ninja gave a cry of shocked dismay. "No! I will not be denied my revenge!"

Scowling furiously, he dug frantically in the bottom of the box, holding up a rapid succession of fragments to the yellow lamplight, as he rejected each one as unreadable. Finally he discovered a section that was more or less intact. But would it be of any use?

Kyodai stared at the small piece for a long time, until a ferocious grin spread slowly on his face beneath the mask. He pulled a flat wallet from his jacket, slid the fragment carefully inside, and slipped it back into his pocket.

Ten minutes had passed since he had found

the entrance to the cave, he reflected—ten minutes to obtain the secret of a lifetime.

The small spark of light hurried back down the slope of the dark mountain. Above, the crater sent up a plume of black smoke over the pulsing glow of red and orange.

Half an hour later, a second dark figure toiled up the flank of Kajiiki and found his way to the small cavern.

Batman stood cautiously behind the white beam of a flashlight. He shone the light to the right and the left, satisfying himself that no one was waiting in ambush. Then he moved into the cave's interior. The signs of recent occupancy were obvious. He walked to the far wall. The white beam glided quickly over the rocks and came to rest on the small opening. Batman stared down at the discarded chest and its cargo of scattered fragments.

29

Bruce Wayne and Master Yoru stood together in the dojo, gazing down at a small table on which the surviving fragments of the ruined scroll had been spread like an ancient jigsaw puzzle.

"I can read only bits and pieces, *Sensei*," Bruce said. "Not enough to understand the techniques of the art. It is fortunate that age has destroyed the dangerous secrets of *kiba-no-hoko*."

"Perhaps not all of them, my friend." Yoru pointed solemnly at a sizeable gap near the edge of the reconstructed scroll. "See there? A large fragment is missing between these two pieces. It is the part that instructs one in the location and performance of the *o-nemuri*—the Death Touch, Bruce-*san*. Perhaps it was reduced to dust, but I do not think so." He turned to look up at the other man's face. "I think that our masked friend is now in grave danger."

Bruce said nothing, his eyes on the gap in the scroll.

30

awn was advancing on Mount Kajiiki, as the sun goddess, Ama-terasu, gazed down upon the land of her people.

The mountain rumbled fiercely as the sun climbed into the sky, as if greeting an old acquaintance—or challenging an old adversary. The red-orange glow was now visible even in the daylight.

Inside the Koruhawa Ward Seismic Monitoring Station some distance from the volcano, a pair of technicians watched the glowing crater through a large window. They exchanged glances as the rumble came again—and with it a tremor that rattled the windows. A third technician stood by a seismograph on the other side of the room, his eyes wide.

Suddenly slender needles danced on the device's turning drum.

The third technician jumped as if touched by a live wire. He darted across the room and snatched a red telephone receiver from its cradle. He pounded the wall impatiently with his fist until the call went through.

"Yes! This is Yoshi Hiro at Station One reporting to Gotojin Headquarters!" The young man spoke rapidly, his voice verging on hysteria. "You must evacuate everyone in the area! The monster has awakened—Great Kajiiki is alive once more!"

The taller of the two techs who stood at the window raised an eyebrow at her colleague. " 'The monster has awakened'?" she repeated in a whisper to the other technician. "Do you ever get the feeling Yoshi-*san* watches too many old movies?"

31

"They say Kajiiki's been acting up again," Mari
Moto told Dick when he met her at the pa-
vilion on the second day of the tournament.
"It's all over this morning's news." She had
the delicate earphones of a miniature
Walkman clasped loosely around her neck.

"Kajiiki?" Dick was mystified. "Never heard
of her. Who is she—a local rock star?"

Mari made a face at him. "*It's* a volcano—
Mount Kajiiki—up north a bit, near Gotojin. Isn't
that where your friends are staying? Why do you
look so tired? Aren't you sleeping well?"

"Volcano, huh?" Dick looked concerned.
"My friends have rooms at the Gotojin Grand Imperator. Do you think they're in any danger?"

"Only if they plan to go hiking on its slopes.
Do you want to go inside now? They should be
starting soon."

"Well, to tell you the truth, I'm kind of hun-
gry." He raised his hands to her, palm out. "And
before you suggest it, I don't even want to *think*
about having raw eel for breakfast. Isn't there any
kind of fast food place around here where I could

get something greasy and reasonably overcooked for a change?"

They ate their morning meal under golden arches a few blocks from the pavilion. "So what's your learned opinion of the tournament so far?" Dick asked around a mouthful of French fries and ketchup.

Mari shrugged. "Some of them are good players. I don't really pay much attention to the individual ratings. I like trying to figure out who's going to win and how long it will take."

"A born oddsmaker, huh? What about the games themselves? Aren't you interested in picking up pointers?"

"There's not too much for me to pick up," she said soberly. Mari drew on the straw in her chocolate shake for a few seconds. "Oh, every once in a great while you come across some really exquisite *tesuji*—that's an absolutely perfect tactical move that nobody sees coming—but these days I go to matches mostly for the aesthetics of the game, the sound of a stone applied correctly to the kaya wood, the geometry of line and circle —" She broke off and lowered her head over her fish sandwich, her cheeks reddening. "Stop looking at me like that!"

"I can't believe you're only fourteen years old," Dick said. "Is it really true—are you *that* good at this game?"

"Fifteen," she said. "Last month. And I'm good enough that I'll never be able to play professionally, no matter how much *Sensei* Hideo wheedles and digs at me. It wouldn't be fair." She turned to look out the wide window at a group of small children chasing one another on hands and knees through a brightly colored maze of plastic tubing in the small recreation area that was attached to the restaurant. "When I play go, I never lose."

"Wait a minute. You mean—"

"Correction. Since the age of six when I played my first game against a serious opponent, I have never lost. Except when I wanted to."

"Why would you ever want to?" Dick took a sip of his Coke, baffled. "I *love* to win—winning is great!"

"Not when you're six years old and everybody's already labeling you a major geek," Mari said quietly. "Not when people get mad at you and claim you're a fake, and reporters follow you around. Not when what you really want to be doing is chasing your friends through big red plastic tubes."

"I see," Dick said after a long moment. "So you don't let on how good you are."

"Not to most people. Suki knows, and one of my friends, but nobody else—not my parents, not Hideo." She finished her sandwich and began folding the empty foil wrapper into a series of diminishing rectangles. "It gets to be almost as much fun as winning: fooling everybody, and doing it just right so they think you're good without being a freak."

"How are your grades?"

"Good," she said, "but not freaky. How are yours?"

"Pretty good." He waggled his hand above the plastic tabletop. "I do best in the subjects I'm interested in. But I get bored too quickly. I'm better at physical stuff—you know, action, movement."

She nodded. "That's why I was surprised when you said you were interested in the go tournament. I figured you'd be into sumo wrestling, like most *gai-jin*."

"Yeah, but go can be exciting, too. Only, not for three whole days." He leaned forward and lowered his voice. "See, one reason I said I wanted to go to the tournament is so Alfred and Bruce would agree to bring me along." He hesitated, then shrugged. "There's a chance Bruce'll need my help while he's over here, only I know he'd never let himself ask for it. Maybe he'll be okay on his own, but maybe not. I just didn't want to risk it, so I got myself included in the trip."

Mari gave him a crooked smile. "So, you do like games of strategy, after all. Just not on a little wooden board."

Dick gave a rueful laugh. "I guess so."

She was studying his face. "And that's why you look so sleepy this morning. You were up all night looking out for your friend."

"Hey." He drew back. "Who told you that?"

"Nobody." Her face reddened again as her fingers folded and refolded the foil wrapper. "I told you I can figure things out. People, too. That's what I do when I watch a match. I observe the players for a little while, and then I know for sure what moves they're going to make."

Dick was watching her with his head tilted to one side. "It's like a superpower," he said at last.

"A real, honest-to-goodness superpower. You could do stuff with that someday. Help people, solve crimes."

She made a skeptical noise. "What? You mean like the Gray Ghost?"

Dick snorted. "The Gray Ghost is an old TV character. He's not real. I was thinking more along the lines of, oh, say—Batman, or Robin."

Mari gave him her one-sided smile again. "I bet you were," she said. She hopped to her feet and swept the litter from their breakfast onto a tray, then carried the tray to the trash can. "Come on, I'm getting really tired of the smell of deep-fried air. Let's go put in an appearance at the tournament."

32

Bruce Wayne sat shirtless, his legs crossed, on the mat on the floor of his compact hotel room. Incense smoke curled lazily toward the ceiling. The room shook slightly as a small quake rumbled beneath the hotel. Bruce remained deep in meditation, a rare expression of serenity on his features.

"Another temblor, Master Bruce."

Bruce's eyes snapped open as Alfred appeared in the adjoining doorway. "The radio is urging people to stay clear of the base of the mountain." The butler checked his watch. "You may wish to take that into account if you still intend to visit Master Yoru at his dojo this afternoon."

"Thank you, Alfred. Perhaps I'll postpone my visit till tomorrow."

"Shall I confirm the flight for our return to Gotham City at the end of the week? Master Dick will be finished with his tournament in another day."

Bruce shook his head. "Not just yet, I'm afraid, old friend."

Alfred had a look of mild surprise on his prim

features. "I had assumed that with the recovery of the young lady and the destruction of the scroll, your chores here were concluded. Even if the mysterious individual who has been investigating your whereabouts turns out to be Kyodai, he must realize that you will defeat him in hand-to-hand combat as easily as you did in the States."

"It hasn't turned out to be that simple, Alfred. The rules have been changed. Yoru *Sensei* has reason to believe that the Ninja got away with the part of the scroll that describes the *o-nemuri* touch."

Alfred frowned. "I'm afraid my Japanese is still a bit rusty in certain areas, Master Bruce."

"It means 'Big Sleep,'" Bruce said grimly. "Though a better translation might be 'Eternal Sleep.'"

"Eternal Sleep." Alfred looked thoughtful, then startled. "Oh," he said. "Oh, my."

The room trembled around them.

Kyodai Ken kneeled on a tattered cushion in his small dojo in a soot-choked section of the Uramachi District. He was hunched over a low table that was illuminated by a single white candle in a cracked jade holder. The wall above the table was dominated by a large poster of a leering dragon executed in sweeping brush strokes. It was the same dragon that Kyodai Ken had had drawn with needles into the flesh of his back.

The lone fragment of parchment he had been able to recover from the box lay on the table. On the faded scrap was the faint outline of a human figure drawn in ink, its interior filled with a thin tracery of *ki* lines in complicated patterns. Instructions written in crabbed *kanji* ran vertically down one side of the drawing. Kyodai studied the writing intently, a look of wary wonder on his face in the candlelight.

"Who would ever have guessed it to be there?" he murmured to himself. His face split in a broad grin. "Oh, I have you now, Wayne!" he exulted with an ugly laugh. "And you, too, Spirit of the Bat!"

He turned and looked across the room to where a human-shaped punching dummy hung on a wire from a hook in the ceiling. Ki lines identical to those on the fragment crisscrossed its soiled canvas surface. Kyodai stood and moved toward the dummy, which swayed slightly in the breeze from outside. He stiffened the first two fingers on his right hand and jabbed lightly at the canvas hide. Then he laughed again.

"I cannot tell you the exact location of the Death Touch point," Yoru told Bruce on the telephone. "I never allowed myself to read the scroll, for fear I might someday be tempted to use the forbidden knowledge."

"It could be anywhere, then," Bruce said.

Yoru nodded. "On the arm, the leg, the back of a hand—your Batman could employ a simple defensive block against one of Kyodai's strikes and find that he has made a fatal error."

Bruce nodded into the telephone. "My business will take me out of town tomorrow," he told the old master. "After my meeting, I'm planning to spend some time at Lake Garabui in the mountain resort area. I've made very certain that anyone who calls inquiring about my schedule will be given that information. Kyodai knows it will be next to impossible for him to locate Batman. If he's the one who's been calling about my schedule—and if he's willing to settle for confronting Bruce Wayne—this should give him ample opportunity."

33

ick and Mari Moto attended the final day of the go tournament. Dick sat in awe as his young companion correctly predicted move after move on each of the four tables. They took a lunch break at noon, and Dick made a brief phone call after they had finished eating. "It's getting boring," Mari told him when he rejoined her at the bench outside the pavilion. "Don't you feel like looking at something other than a go board while you're in Japan?"

"Sure. As a matter of fact . . ." He checked his wristwatch. "Have you ever heard of a place called Lake Garabui? I heard it was real nice this time of year, and I was kind of planning to head out there this afternoon." He fumbled in his jacket pocket for a map inscribed with microscopic print. He spread it on the bench. *"If* I can find the place. My directional sense doesn't seem to be functioning all that well in your country. It's probably the raw fish."

"Garabui?" She refolded the map for him and stuffed it back into his pocket. "I could find it blindfolded. My family used to go there all the time. It's near Hakone, which is a big mountain resort area." She looked sideways at him. "We could leave after I check in at home—unless you're tired of hanging around with a fourteen-year-old."

Dick smiled. "Fifteen last month," he reminded her. "To tell you the truth, I've been having a great time. It's not bad having a little sister."

They started their journey on the *Nozomi,* the fastest of the bullet trains. While the countryside sped by, Mari compiled a list of things to do once they reached the mountains.

"First we should check out the sculpture garden at the open-air museum in Hakone. Then we can take the world's second-longest tramway over Mount Komagatake. There are volcanic springs to see and lots of souvenir shops. Do you read comic books? My friend Toku has a huge collection. We have mostly *manga* over here, but I enjoy American ones when I can get them. Let's see . . ." She touched the tip of her pencil to her tongue. "We should definitely ride a swan boat when we get to Lake Garabui. It's the kind of touristy thing that people get upset with you if you don't do while you're there."

Dick had his nose buried in the English/Japanese phrasebook Alfred had given him. He had been muttering softly while Mari went over her list. Now he lifted his head and carefully pronounced a long string of Japanese words. "Okay," he said at the end. "What did I say?"

Mari rolled her eyes. "You told me that your name was Mr. Smith and that you and your friend Mr. Bernard were both diplomats from France.

Then you said that you had asked for peach blossoms and not cherry blossoms." She sighed. "Satisfied?"

"Neat!" Dick grinned. "Communication has been established." He lowered his head into the phrasebook again.

When they reached the mountains, they left the bullet train and found themselves in a picturesque town filled with little shops. They walked on flat wooden bridges, steam rising on either side of them, as Mari led them on an exploration of some of the hot springs that dotted the region. Dick spouted phrases from his book, and the springs hissed in response.

They boarded a smaller train to begin their ascent up the steeper slopes, eventually arriving at the mountain known as Komagatake. The world's second-longest tramway brought them a view of Mount Fuji Dick recognized from dozens of postcards, and then deposited them not far from Lake Garabui.

Dick stood and gazed out over the calm expanse of blue water. Those swan boats not in use sat tethered in a double row on either side of a long pier stretching out into the lake. The pier was hung with brightly colored lights on a score of tall, thin poles that swayed in the light breeze. Small loudspeakers were hidden among the lights, and delicate music rippled out across the lake.

Dick decided that the boats really did look like giant waterfowl from a distance. He inspected the nearest one, discovering that they seated four people and were covered with a tentlike cabin constructed of white canvas stretched on a round frame. A neck and head assembly of carved and painted wood completed the illusion. Dick and Mari took a short ride in one, then settled back in a pair of deck chairs and watched successive groups of tourists do the same.

"Want to play Frisbee?" Mari hefted the compact backpack she had picked up at her parents' house. She opened a zipper and pulled out a worn black plastic disk.

They tossed the Frisbee back and forth for close to an hour. Dick was impressed by Mari's performance. She managed to capture the disk with a minimum of running back and forth, always seeming to know where it was going to glide before Dick threw it. Dick specialized in entertaining catches, topped by a triple spin in midair that had several spectators applauding him. Finally they collapsed back in their deck chairs.

"I want to learn how to do things like that," Mari panted.

"You're doing great," Dick told her. "You've got wonderful hand-eye coordination."

"But I don't have any flair, like you do. And I need to build some muscle. Catching's easy, but I want to catch it like nobody else does. And I need to be able to throw it farther than a few yards." She pursed her lips and stared out over the lake. "I need a super-hero *sensei* to show me the ropes."

"I think you're right." Dick nodded. "But first you'll need a flashy costume and a dramatic name. In fact, a catchy name is the most important part of being a super-hero. Let's see—" He gnawed on his thumbnail. "I've got it—Logic

Lass! Or Strategy Woman? How about the unbeatable Go Girl!"

Mari folded her arms on her chest. "Now
you're making fun of me again," she said.

"What, you don't like Go Girl? No accounting
for taste." Dick shrugged and pulled out his
phrasebook.

"Hey," Mari said after a few minutes.
"There's a frozen yogurt stand over there. Want
one?"

"Depends. What are they serving today?"

"I can't see the specials from here, but I'm
hoping for triple chocolate fudge."

"Gee, that sounds awfully normal. I would
have thought you'd prefer something a little more
exotic—like fish egg crunch or eel ripple."

"Eel yogurt?" Mari wrinkled up her face.
"You foreigners sure have some weird ideas."

Dick took advantage of Mari's absence to carefully survey the lakeside. Almost immediately, he
spotted Bruce Wayne strolling along the shore
with his suit jacket slung over his shoulder, the
picture of an off-duty executive. Dick ducked
down behind his phrasebook as Mari returned
with two Styrofoam bowls, shifting his body so
that she blocked him from view.

"Here." Mari handed him his bowl. "I got
your favorite."

Dick inspected the frozen confection with
skepticism. He took a spoonful of pale green and
white and brought it to his lips. His face lit up
with surprised delight. "Hey! Pistachio and coco-
nut with peanut butter chips. How'd you guess?"

Mari shrugged. "How did I guess Hashime

would force a *ko* fight for his corner near the end of that match this morning?" she replied. "Because that's the way Hashime plays the game."

"You're a little scary sometimes, you know that?" Dick glanced past her at the shore, then pulled his head back.

Mari turned to follow his gaze, turning back with a small frown. "So what do you want to do now?" she asked when they had finished their desserts. "I'm ready to do some exploring."

"Oh, not me." Dick patted his waist with a theatrical yawn. "I just want to lie here for a while and absorb all these calories."

"Fine—be a vegetable," Mari grumbled as she got to her feet. "I'm going for a walk." She left with a muttered comment about the "older generation" and headed toward a row of shops located halfway around the lake.

Perfect, Dick thought. He settled back behind his phrasebook and tried to figure out what Bruce was up to. It seemed that he was being deliberately conspicuous, as if he were trying to lure someone out of hiding. Dick craned his neck above the book as Bruce made his way out onto the long pier and began speaking to the swan boat attendant. Dick's jaw dropped. Drifting around in a boat shaped like a big white bird didn't seem like something Bruce Wayne would find entertaining under the best of circumstances. No one else was out on the lake. If he wants to be conspicuous, Dick mused to himself, this is a pretty good way to go about it.

He watched as Bruce paid the attendant and slid under the white canopy of one of the boats.

The little gas motor sputtered to life seconds later, and the simulated swan chugged away from the pier.

Bruce kept his hand lightly on the tiller, steering the boat into a wide looping course that repeatedly brought it back near the long pier. He had paid the attendant enough for an uninterrupted hour on the water, tipping him heavily to allow him to go out without someone else in the boat. Several others took boats out and returned them while he circled lazily. The sky began to grow gradually darker until the attendant threw a switch and the pier suddenly blazed with colored lights. There appeared to be something wrong with one of the strands of wire; the lights flickered and blinked for several minutes before finally staying on.

It was nearing the end of Bruce's hour. He was several hundred yards out in the water at the far end of his latest loop. A heavyset blond couple, obviously tourists, made their way onto the pier and approached the attendant, who was busy refueling one of the tiny vessels. They discussed terms with the man, paid him, and stepped into the boat. Bruce watched as the attendant leaned forward to untie the mooring line. The woman had moved to the back of the boat beneath the white canopy. She started the small engine too soon and the giant swan lurched against the pier. The attendant leaned under the canopy to caution her just as the boat gave another sharp lurch and butted the edge of the dock. Bruce's eyes narrowed in the growing dimness as he saw a red gasoline can teeter on the edge of the wooden planks and tip over. Liquid gushed onto the back of the white craft.

"Hey!" Bruce cupped his hands around his mouth and called to them, but the engine noise kept them from hearing him. He gunned his own motor and started in toward the dock. Just then the portly blond man stepped near the prow of the rocking swan and leaned down with one foot on the pier to help the attendant unfasten the mooring line. He stood up just as the boat leaped away from the dock, lost his footing on the smooth hull, and hopped back onto the planks, reaching out with a hand to steady himself against one of the fragile poles that held the strings of colored lights.

The pole swayed wildly, and Bruce saw one of the wires pull away from its fastenings up above. The blond man looked up and stumbled away from the pole, backing directly into the one behind it. The second pole lashed the air, knocking loose a small loudspeaker. The lights flickered as the speaker dragged a strand of wire above the swan boat, which was still butting helplessly against the pier as the woman fought with the tiller. A pair of wires crossed and a small shower of sparks rained down, just missing the gas-soaked vessel. Another loop of lights came loose.

"No!" Bruce cast about wildly in the dim light, looking for some way to intervene. Out of the corner of his eye, he saw something dark glide out over the water behind him, coming to rest with a gentle bump against the swan boat's prow. Bruce scooped the black disk up from the water and turned to sight along the lake to the pier. He reared back in the boat and let the Frisbee fly. The saucer shape hurtled through the air.

The Frisbee found its mark, the edge of the black disk slamming into the switch Bruce had seen the attendant flip earlier. Power to the wires was cut off just as a final hook gave way and the mass of lights came down on top of the gasoline-covered swan boat.

Half a dozen attendants were crowded around the blond couple as Bruce guided his own boat up to the pier several minutes later. One of them left the group long enough to help Bruce moor his swan.

"Some excitement while I was out?" Bruce asked in Japanese.

"*Hai.*" The man nodded. "Some gasoline spilled onto their boat. Then the lights came down. Luckily, the main switch must have been loose. It fell into the off position, cutting off all power to the lines just before they touched the gas. A few lightbulbs were broken, nothing more." He shook his head in the direction of the agitated tourists. "Those *gai-jin* do not realize how close they came to never seeing their home in Düsseldorf again."

Bruce strolled along the pier until he found the black Frisbee, which he scooped up and concealed beneath his jacket. He looked shoreward in the waning light, scanning the deck chairs he had noticed earlier. They were empty.

"I still don't see why we had to leave so suddenly," Mari said grumpily as she and Dick rode the tramway back over the top of Mount Koma-gatake. "And what was all that fuss over by the swan boats?"

"Oh, a couple of tourists were having trouble getting their sea legs," Dick told her. "Anyway, I'd had enough relaxation for one afternoon. I was hoping we'd make it back to Kyoto in time for the Godzilla film festival. I think it would be neat to see it with the American voices dubbed in for a change." He raised his phrasebook and re-cited a rapid string of syllables.

Mari settled back into her seat with a sigh of resignation. "Yes, Mr. Bernard," she responded dutifully. "I know you ordered peach blossoms for the French ambassador." She straightened suddenly, checking the padded seat to either side of her. "Hey! What happened to my Frisbee?"

34

Alfred had risen early and made his way to the farmer's market located not far from the hotel. The large, open-air marketplace attracted consumers from all over the city, and at this hour it was crowded with sights and sounds. Alfred strolled contentedly down the rows of produce and fresh fish, purchasing an occasional item of exceptional quality and dropping it into his rattan basket. He towered over many of the local tradespeople, ramrod straight and every inch the British butler in his white linens and panama hat.

Behind Alfred came another tall man. Dressed as a fishmonger, he took great pains to remain unnoticed as he kept his eye on the Englishman. Whenever the butler chanced to glance behind him, the man would suddenly become interested in a display of squid or freshly caught lingcod on ice.

Alfred's mind was focused on the dinner he was planning to prepare on the small stove provided in their suite. Oblivious of the surveillance, he paused at the stall of a one-eyed farmer and hefted a juicy-looking tomato. He pursed his lips, eyeing the vegetable critically as he held it up in front of the farmer. "Excuse me, honored madam," he inquired in his formal Japanese, "but was this splendid red giant organically grown?"

Behind him, the tall fishmonger watched from beneath his wide-brimmed hat.

35

The phone began to ring as Bruce was unlocking the door to the suite. He checked his watch. "Alfred?" He stuck his head through the doorway to the adjoining room, then returned, frowning, to pick up the receiver. "Hello? Alfred?"

His question was answered by a burst of familiar, harsh-sounding laughter. "No, rich man. But he is here with me. Where have you been all day? Your manservant and I have been trying to reach you."

"Kyodai." A chill fluttered up Bruce's spine. He kept his voice even with an effort. "Let me speak to Alfred."

"Well, you may speak to him all you like, Wayne-*san*, but I fear he will have difficulty answering." Kyodai turned from the phone as if directing his comments to someone nearby. "Your master wishes proof of your well-being, manservant. Can I persuade you to assure him that you are being well treated here?" Bruce's jaw tightened as he heard the sound of a brief struggle, followed by a muffled groan of pain.

"I am afraid he is not feeling very talkative at the moment, Wayne-*san*. Perhaps it is because of the wad of silk I had to insert in his mouth when I grew weary of his *Igirisu-jin* chattering." Kyodai's malevolent smile was evident in his voice.

"What do you want, Kyodai? Tell me now."

"You are in no position to make demands, Wayne-*san*," the Ninja replied sullenly. "Besides, there are so many things that I want in this world. Perhaps you would like to wait until I have drawn up a complete list of them. But, no, I will be satisfied with one small request." His joking manner gave way to sudden steel. "You will face me, rich man," he said in a ringing voice, "as yourself, or as your alter ego, it is all one to me—but you *will* face me! Old Yoru will tell you when and where." He severed the connection.

In the suite at the Gotojin Grand Imperator, Bruce lowered the phone slowly into its cradle. He looked down. Fastened to the base of the telephone was a small electronic instrument with a number pad that Bruce had attached as a precaution on the night of his arrival. As he watched, an LCD screen on the side of the box began to flash with digits. A phone number. Bruce touched the tiny keypad with his fingertips and held his breath. An address began to scroll across the screen:

536 TEZUKA

Bound hand and foot, his arms stretched painfully over his head by a taut wire strung from a

hook in the ceiling, Alfred Pennyworth inspected
Kyodai Ken's dojo at 536 Tezuka Lane with a
feeling of regret. Several minutes earlier, just before the Ninja had placed his call to the hotel,
Alfred had regained consciousness and become instantly aware of the fact that he had failed his
friend. Through his foolishness in allowing himself to be taken prisoner by this individual, he had
created a situation in which Master Bruce's life
would soon be placed in the gravest danger. To
make matters worse, he had awakened with a
pounding headache.

The tautness of the wire kept him standing so
straight that the soles of his shoes barely made
contact with the floor. It also prevented him from
turning his body any appreciable amount to either
side. By craning his neck, he could see that he had
been suspended next to a *makawara* practice
dummy whose body was covered with a tracery of
ki lines. He wondered if this deliberate juxtaposi-
tion of prisoner and dummy was Kyodai's idea of
a joke.

The Ninja had been standing in front of Alfred
with his back to the other man while he finished
his phone conversation with Bruce Wayne. Now
Kyodai turned and stalked toward the butler.
Stopping directly in front of the bound figure, he
drew his arm back, laughing as Alfred flinched
slightly in response. Moving slightly to the right,
Kyodai jabbed sharply at the practice dummy with
stiffened fingers. Alfred twisted his neck, trying in
vain to see where the Ninja's fingers contacted the
dummy.

"A single touch," Kyodai sneered. "Can you believe it? That is all that will be required to destroy your master!"

Alfred closed his eyes. His headache was getting worse.

36

The phone had started to ring again just as Bruce was preparing to leave the suite for Yoru's dojo. He snatched the receiver eagerly from the cradle, his mind filled with the wild hope that his old friend had somehow managed to free himself from his captor and was calling to report that he was out of harm's way. His heart sank when he heard Dick's voice on the other end of the line.

"Hey, how's it going? Has Kajiki blown his cork yet?"

"Everything's fine here, Dick." Bruce found himself resenting the cheerful undertone in Dick's voice, and had difficulty keeping the brusqueness out of his voice. "You caught me on my way out the door. I'm about to leave for an important appointment."

"Okay, partner, no problem. I won't keep you. Is Alfred there—or will he be going with you? I wanted to see if he felt like meeting me at the train station later this evening. Now that the tournament's over, I thought I might as well head back to Gotojin and take it easy with you guys, instead of spending the night here by myself. I'm kind of looking forward to a long hot shower in a private bathroom."

"Alfred's already gone out," Bruce said. "I think it would be better for you to stay in Kyoto till tomorrow morning, as we'd planned. Neither Alfred nor myself will have any time to meet your train tonight."

"Well, I could always hop a cab—"

"Dick, you agreed to follow the itinerary we set up for you." Bruce glanced at his watch. "Now *follow* it!" he replaced the receiver on the cradle and left the room.

"So what's the word?" Mari watched his face curiously as Dick stepped from the phone booth. "Not good, huh?"

Dick shook his head. "Not good at all. Want to walk me to the train station?"

"Stop by my folks' house and I'll do better than that. I was supposed to take the bullet in and stay at Suki's apartment for the weekend. Let me pick up a few things and I'll ride in with you now."

"But your parents—"

"I'll tell my folks it's okay with Suki for me to get there a day early—which it will be, once I've told her it's okay with our parents. Simple. And you get to tell me more about the aesthetics of double back flips."

Dick thought about his own reasons for going to Gotojin ahead of schedule. His sense of unease had been confirmed by Bruce's tone during the conversation. Chances were, he would need to begin tracking his secretive friend as soon as he reached the city. "Look, I'm probably going to have things to do, once we—"

Mari threw her hands up in annoyance. "Oh, don't worry, I'm not planning on tagging along and ruining whatever fascinating evening you had planned." Suddenly she seemed like a perfectly ordinary, if somewhat sulky, fifteen-year-old. "I just thought it would be fun to hang out together on the train for one last time. Once we get to the station, I'll go straight to my sister's." She checked her watch. "There's a Gray Ghost rerun that comes on about eight. I never miss the chance to watch a *real* hero in action."

"Well . . ." He was almost convinced. "I guess if it's all right with your parents. But are you sure it's safe for you to be roaming the city by yourself?"

"Piece of cake." She waved her hand in a gesture of dismissal. "I know Gotojin real well. Now come on." She slipped her arm through his and urged him away from the phone booth. "We've got to hurry if we want to catch the six o'clock. Remember—timing is everything."

Dick allowed himself to be guided down the street with only a trace of reluctance. After all, he reasoned, he was about to break the rules himself. How could he be upset with someone else for merely bending them?

It seemed no time at all before the two friends were saying their farewells in the Gotojin station. "Thanks for everything," Dick said, leaning down to give Mari a hug. "Keep up the good work. You'll be a super-hero before you know it. Oh, and I'll be sending you a new Frisbee as soon as I get home, to replace the one I lost at the lake."

"Great," Mari said. "Try to find one with the Gray Ghost logo." She glanced at her wristwatch as Dick headed off into the evening after a final hug. Not bad. If she hurried, she could make it to her sister's apartment in time for the early rerun. She left the station and turned down a side street, automatically choosing the safest route through the bustling city, where she would be least likely to run into any trouble.

And if something unforeseen did occur? She felt reassuringly at her waist. In addition to a tiny cellular phone, she also carried an extremely loud whistle, a small spray bottle filled with a potent mixture of her own creation, and her recently attained black belt in karate.

Mari Moto smiled to herself as she melted into the shadows at the edge of the street. One way or another, the unbeatable Go Girl was on the road to becoming a force to be reckoned with.

Bruce had found Yoru *Sensei*'s dojo deserted when he arrived. Feeling as though he were back in his student days, he changed into the familiar white *gi* and pants, drew the black belt around his waist, and began practicing a series of difficult katas while he waited for his old mentor to appear. As he worked, he pushed the importance of tonight's battle out of his mind, centering his thoughts on the movements themselves until his brain and his body blended into a seamless entity. His katas were razor sharp; the stiff canvas *gi* made popping sounds as he threw chops and punches with blurring speed. He made a final leap through the air, landed, and stood erect. Then he bowed to an imaginary instructor.

Pulling off his belt, he draped it around his neck and headed toward the changing room.

Kairi was standing in the doorway.

"Yoru *Sensei* is resting at his home," she said softly. "He is an old man, though his pupils do not like to admit that to themselves. The past few days have been very difficult for him." She flexed her shoulders beneath her training jacket. "He gave me a message for you. 'Nine o'clock, just below the cave.' He said that you would understand." She looked up at him with concern. "Is there anything you need? Food? Company?"

"No," he replied in Japanese. "Thank you. I am fine."

"Given two roads, you tend to choose the solitary path, do you not, Wayne-*san*?" She was studying his face thoughtfully. "That must be a lonely way at times."

He shrugged. "It is the way I have always gone. The best way for me."

"Perhaps." She shifted her gaze to Kajiiki, visible as a smoking beacon through the far window. "Will you fight Kyodai?" she asked.

"I am not the one to answer that question." Bruce followed her gaze. "It is the Batman that Kyodai wishes to face."

Kairi nodded once in understanding. "And will you be able to persuade this Batman to fight the Ninja?"

"Batman does as he wishes," Bruce said carefully. "But I am certain he will wish to meet Kyodai Ken in battle."

"As am I. This costumed one would have made a great samurai," Kairi mused softly, her dark eyes on Bruce.

"Perhaps he is more ninja than samurai," Bruce suggested with a wry smile. "I must go now." He moved past her into the changing room.

"Good luck," Kairi said quietly.

Evening shadows painted the streets in shades of blue and black as a caped figure moved silently across a series of rooftops, slipping from shadow to lengthening shadow. The neon was just beginning to flicker on along Tezuka Lane as he scaled the wall of a shabby-looking building and climbed onto its roof.

A skylight was at the center of the rooftop of Kyodai Ken's small dojo. One pane had been broken and replaced with a sheet of plywood at some point in the past. The Dark Knight peered through the rectangle of dusty glass that remained. His fingers worked the latch, then he carefully lifted the window on its hinges. He dropped noiselessly to the floor and spun in a quick circle inside the darkened room, his long cape flaring. There were no signs of life.

He noticed the practice dummy still dangling on its wire from the ceiling, and strode to stand before it. His mouth drew down at the corners as he saw the second strand of wire hanging from the other hook.

Batman turned deliberately from the wire and

began to examine the dummy. He looked closely at the *ki* lines, tracing one of them along the simulated torso with his gloved forefinger. He stopped at a junction point near the center of the body, picked up another *ki* line with his fingertip, and moved slowly down at an angle to the first. His face took on a thoughtful look.

37

The wind blew with a cutting edge above the dark slope. The volcano called Mount Kajiiki was restive to the point of violence. Smoke billowed from its crown and lava shot upward in glowing geysers.

Batman found the Ninja standing near the mouth of the cave, legs wide and hands on hips in an unconsciously dramatic pose. The Dark Knight surveyed the area from behind a jut of rock on slightly higher ground, shifting position gradually until he located Alfred. The butler sat propped up against a rocky wall beneath a jutting overhang, his slender figure managing to maintain its air of dignity despite the ropes that still bound him hand and foot.

Batman stepped out from behind the spar. Pebbles raced each other down the slope as he moved into view and started down to meet his enemy.

"Ah." Kyodai Ken raised his chin to the gray-clad figure. "The game resumes!" he said with relish. Beneath his mask, the Ninja's face split in a broad grin. He raised his arm and pointed to the fiery summit, where plumes of incandescent lava shot fifty feet into the night sky. "How do you like our fire breather, *gai-jin*? Impressive, is he not?"

"Very."

"Once again you approach unseen, Dark One." Kyodai bowed slightly in appreciation. "You would have made a good ninja."

"I would prefer to be a samurai," Batman replied. He paused on a small terrace a few feet above the flat area where the Ninja stood.

"But you are like me, a warrior of the night," the other man persisted.

"Did you ask me here to talk, Ninja?"

Kyodai laughed. "I asked you here to finish the game once and for all, to dance death with me this night."

"And are you planning to leave the dance early, as you did the last time?" Batman inquired drily.

The Ninja's smile curdled. "When I leave will not matter one bit to you, little bat." He spread his hands. "Once you have felt the dragon's fang, you will no longer care anything for what happens in this world."

Batman completed his descent and faced the Ninja on level ground. His eyes flicked to Alfred, flicked away. The older man seemed to be conscious and in relatively sound condition, despite his rough treatment. "I know about the scroll," he said quietly. "And about what you have learned."

The Ninja's eyes widened a fraction. "So much the better." He made an impatient gesture that included Alfred. "The time for talk is long past. Come, fight me now—or the *Igirisu-jin* servant pays the price for your cowardice."

The two men assumed martial stances and drifted toward one another, circling warily. They had fought before, but this time was different, and the change was apparent in their movements. The man in black was armed with a new weapon: his knowledge of how to inflict the Death Touch. He moved with an assurance that approached arrogance.

The Ninja gave a short bark of laughter. Then he lifted his hand to his head and pulled off his mask with a sudden flourish. Kyodai Ken's sardonic grin flashed in the light from the volcano.

"Let us face each other as men, one to another," he taunted the Dark Knight. "Are you not samurai? Samurai do not hide behind masks."

Batman hesitated. Then, slowly, he removed his cape and cowl and lay them to one side on the rough stone. "Very well."

As the Dark Knight was turning back, the Ninja leaped forward in his first attack. Batman dodged and launched a counterattack, his nerves and muscles responding without hesitation to the messages brought by his senses. Kyodai fell back, circled, sprang forward again. The small plateau was filled with a blur of black and gray motion composed of feints, lunges, quick steps back and forth.

Kyodai grinned as he sensed a slight hesitancy in the Dark Knight's responses. No doubt his enemy's skill was hobbled by the sure knowledge

that to allow Kyodai Ken to come too close might
prove fatal; what followed was indeed a kind of
martial dance, with parries and sidesteps more evident than kicks and punches. "Why do you back
away, night fighter," Kyodai jeered at him.
"Afraid of my gentle touch?"

Mount Kajiiki showed its increasing displeasure with the world as the two battled. The
ground shook violently, quieted, shook again as
volcanic eruptions began to occur more fre-
quently. Kyodai tossed his head in wild approval
after one particularly unsettling quake. "A fitting
backdrop to this final encounter," he exulted
through his tight grin.

"A foolish choice for a battleground," Batman
told him. Small cracks appeared in the dark rock
of the mountainside at their backs as the earth
beneath them began to move in sluggish undula-
tions. "If we stay here, the volcano may claim us
all." He spared another glance at Alfred. The
rocky overhang under which Kyodai had tucked
him seemed sufficient to protect the butler from
the burning cinders that were now beginning to
hurtle down from Kajiiki's peak.

Kyodai Ken spread his arms as he continued to
circle in the warrior's dance. "For myself, I am
quite prepared to die." He made a sudden lunge,
which his foe barely sidestepped on the heaving
ground. "Are you?"

The Dark Knight returned his concentration
to the contest. The fight raged on: savage, con-
trolled—and even. For every attack the Ninja
launched, his opponent brought forth a counter-

move. It soon became apparent to both combatants that neither could overcome the other.

"Enough! It ends now!" In a burst of final determination, Kyodai Ken leapt forward and clinched with Batman. The pair grappled like sumo wrestlers, locked tightly together as they fought a war of strength and leverage. A flame of desperation flared in Kyodai's eyes as the Dark Knight slowly forced him back across the buckling plateau. "You are strong," he grunted, "but not strong enough!" With a cry of rage and triumph, the Ninja drew back his right hand and stabbed his stiffened fingers at Batman.

There was a moment of stillness.

Then Alfred's eyes widened in dismay as the Dark Knight slumped forward against his opponent. Kyodai grinned in delight and slowly relaxed his grip. "At last!" he grated. *"Sayonara,* Batman!"

The triumph faded as Batman suddenly straightened in his opponent's arms. The Dark Knight gripped the Ninja's forearms, whirled, and tossed Kyodai to the ground. The Ninja reacted in astonishment, his concentration shattered. The fabled Death Touch had failed.

"The *o-nemuri*!" he cried in bewilderment. "How could you withstand it? No man is immune!"

"It's all over, Kyodai." Batman stood above him, arms crossed on his chest. "The Death Touch is a sham. It doesn't work."

Alfred leaned back against the heaving rock, his eyes glistening with relief in the orange glow that seemed to fill the night.

The Dark Knight reached down for his defeated foe. Suddenly, the ground convulsed beneath them, splitting open like a grinning mouth and driving them scrambling back from opposite sides of a rapidly widening chasm.

38

atman leaped back as molten rock welled up from the yawning crevice. The ground shuddered again as more fractures ripped it open.

Kyodai Ken was trapped on a rocky spur surrounded by the rising liquid. He crouched by a small boulder on an island hemmed in by lava that bubbled up continuously, forming glowing streams too wide for even the Ninja to leap.

The Dark Knight snatched a Batarang from his belt and hurled it at Kyodai. A thin, strong line trailed from the black batwing. The object landed on the twisting rock at Kyodai's feet.

"Grab it!" Batman called. "If I pull and you jump, you can still make it!"

The lava rose. Kyodai's island haven narrowed rapidly, until only a small strip of dry rocky soil remained. The Ninja stepped up onto the single boulder that protruded from the spit of land. Smoke poured from the glowing rivers, partially obscuring the scene. The wind whipped it away for a moment and Batman could see that his adversary's perch had shrunk to a small bump of gray rock rising from a sea of orange. Flames danced on the lava as vegetation crisped and burned. The boulder started to wobble, its base melting.

"Kyodai! The rope!" Batman stood and watched, his fists clenched helplessly at his sides.

The Ninja looked down at the Batarang lying next to his foot. He kicked it into the lava with the toe of his black slipper. The black wing and the line that trailed from it burst into flame. Kyodai looked up at the Dark Knight, sweat streaming down his face.

"You *are* samurai, after all!" he whispered, a note of wonder in his voice. He bowed to his opponent. Then Kyodai Ken drew himself up to his full height and removed his black shirt. As the rock upon which he stood began to topple into the bubbling river, he turned his back and raised his arms as if in supplication to the mouth of the volcano. The dragon coiled on his back seemed to writhe as more smoke billowed up, blocking Batman's view.

A blast of withering heat forced the Dark Knight to stumble back from the edge of the crevice. When the smoke cleared, the lava was streaming unhindered down the slope.

Batman stared into the melted river of rock, his face expressionless beneath the orange light.

The Dark Knight's discarded cape and cowl burst into flames, burning to ashes before his eyes as the streams of lava split and multiplied.

Batman sprinted across the small plateau, dodging fiery meteors from the summit. He knelt at Alfred's side. The ground shook again, and another fiery chasm split open nearby. He pulled Alfred from beneath the rocky overhang and slung him over his shoulder. He leaped across the new chasm to safety just as the ground he was standing on collapsed into the subterranean inferno. He turned and began to make his way down the blazing slope.

Soon Mount Kajiiki was a sullen red glow in the distance. Batman walked wearily beside Alfred, supporting his old friend against his side. He drew another cowl from his belt and settled it over his head, pulling the mask down over his face as they talked.

"I couldn't see through the smoke. Was Kyodai . . . ?"

"I don't know, Alfred." Batman shook his head. "I wish I did."

39

They found their way to Yoru's dojo and rested for a while. Bruce had left his street clothes in the changing room. He put them on and used the telephone to summon a taxi to take them back into the city. When they arrived at the hotel, they found Dick's loafers sitting neatly side by side outside the door to the suite. Sliding aside the thin partition to his room, they discovered Dick himself sprawled on the futon, apparently deep in slumber.

Alfred brewed a pot of green tea and the two men discussed the night's events in quiet tones in Bruce's room.

"You took a great risk tonight," Alfred told his friend and employer.

Bruce lit a stick of incense and sat staring at the curl of white smoke. Then he shook his head as if awakening from a reverie. "Not really," he replied. He rose to his feet and turned his back. When he turned around again, he held a piece of gray material the size of a small wallet in his hand.

Alfred raised his brows inquiringly.

"High density Kevlar," Bruce explained. "I

found Kyodai's practice dummy in the dojo. When I examined it closely, I discovered a soft spot, a place that had obviously been jabbed many times. I figured there was a strong chance that it marked the location of the Death Touch." He hefted the superstrong material. "So I protected that same place on my own body."

Alfred shook his head in amazement.

40

The next day, Bruce set up meetings for the afternoon to conclude his business with his associates. Then he returned to the dojo to say his good-byes to Master Yoru.

"I'm sorry for what happened to Kyodai Ken," he told his old teacher. "I guess I'll always feel partly responsible for the way he turned out."

"Ultimately, we all choose the paths we walk," Yoru said. "Some lead up the mountain and into the light, others wind down into the dark valley." He studied his former pupil. "The next time you see your Batman, please tell him that I have great respect for him."

"Why?" Bruce was puzzled. "He is as much a ninja as Kyodai was."

"Not so. Batman offered to help his adversary when it was clearly not to his advantage to do so. And we both know that a lesser man would have given in to fear and used the knowledge of the Death Touch against his opponent." The old instructor stepped up to Bruce, gazing directly at him. "Batman is the essence of samurai, Wayne-*san*. You would do well to remember that."

"He learned from a great teacher." Bruce held the old man's gaze. "Thank you, *Sensei*. I will deliver your message. I am sure that Batman will feel honored by your words." He bowed.

Yoru returned his bow. The two men clasped hands.

41

Alfred had left the hotel shortly after Bruce to make arrangements for their flight home that evening. Instead of returning directly to the suite, he treated himself to a final tour of the city, including a lengthy visit to the farmer's market. It was mid-afternoon by the time he arrived back at the room.

When he unlocked the door, he found Dick seated on a tatami in the common room, studying his go board. The butler made a brief sidetrip into his own room, then returned to seat himself on the mat opposite the young man.

Dick nodded in greeting. "I decided to sleep in," he told the butler. "But I saw your note when I got up, so I'm all packed. When do we leave?"

"The limousine will be picking us up in just over an hour. Master Bruce should be returning shortly."

"I kind of hate to go," Dick said. "It's been an interesting visit."

"Indeed," Alfred agreed. He touched the polished surface of the board with his fingertips.

"And have you learned anything new about the game during the past few days, Master Dick?"

"Yeah, lots," Dick replied. "And from the most unlikely people."

"Interesting. And would you care to tell me when you first learned about the real reason for Master Bruce's trip to this country?"

"Real reason?" Dick's cheeks flushed pink. "I'm not sure I know what you mean."

"Perhaps these will refresh your memory." Alfred reached behind his back and brought forth Dick's loafers. "This time they really were in need of cleaning. I took the liberty of bringing them into my room last night and giving them a thorough going over—*before* Master Bruce had the opportunity to notice the large fragments of ash and volcanic rock adhering to their soles."

"Whoops." Dick's face had achieved a uniform redness. "Thanks, Alfred. I owe you one."

"You owe me at least an answer to my previous question, Master Dick." Alfred lifted a white stone from one of the shallow bowls and set it firmly onto the board.

"You know how unpredictable the acoustics are in the Batcave, Alfred," Dick said. "It's not like I was eavesdropping or anything, but I heard Bruce mention Master Yoru, so I knew his reason for coming over here was probably related to the Ninja. I picked up enough clues once we got here to confirm my suspicions. After that, there was no way I could let him face it on his own. I've been more or less shadowing him since we arrived in Gotojin, just in case he needed a hand." Dick gave a philosophical shrug.

"Not exactly the most forthright manner in which to conduct oneself." Alfred's face reflected disapproval.

"Oh, you know how it is, Alfred. You've done the same thing in the past. If we could just count on him to come out and tell us when he needed help, we wouldn't have to play these little games behind his back." Dick dug a black stone from his own bowl and set it next to Alfred's white. He regarded the board thoughtfully. "Hey, look at that move," he said. "I *did* learn something, after all."

Bruce Wayne stood quietly outside the thin door to the suite, a tiny smile on his lips. His thoughts went back to their first night in Gotojin, when he had apprehended Daggett's false ninjas in the middle of their break-in. A flash of familiar movement in the shadows near the limousine had told him that Robin was poised to help if necessary. From then on it had been a simple matter to detect his young friend's hovering presence—in the streets, at the lake, on the mountainside—and to shake his shadow when the situation threatened to be genuinely dangerous.

Bruce patted his briefcase. He had almost considered presenting Dick with the black Frisbee that had appeared so miraculously alongside his swan boat. He shook his head. Better to let his friends think they had outwitted him, at least for the time being. Playing the game made it much easier to keep tabs on their whereabouts and so protect them from harm. And wasn't that the most important thing?

Bruce turned the handle and opened the door.

ABOUT THE AUTHOR

GEARY GRAVEL is the author of *Shadows of the Past* and *Dual to the Death*, based on *Batman: The Animated Series.* He has also written *Mask of the Phantasm*, the novelization of *Batman: The Animated Movie.* His other books include *A Key for the Nonesuch* and *Return of the Breakneck Boys*, the first two volumes of the Fading Worlds series. Strongly committed to the ideal of a well-rounded life, he balances his comic-book reading with healthy doses of TV and movies.